Burn Sizzle Bleed: The Hearts of Others

James P. Johnson lives and works in Denver.
This is his first book.

Published by Snowy Morning Entertainment
Copyright 2007 by James P. Johnson
All rights reserved
ISBN 978-0-6152-0672-1

To
Amy, Tommy, and Shoun...
Your support and enthusiasm
are immeasurable.

It was one of those moments when you hope the moisture between your ass cheeks is just sweat.

I was a bike messenger in Denver for almost five years. It didn't make me rich, but it was honest work and it kept me fed. I rode hard, and I rode year round. I saved a little money and I traveled a little. That was my life.

If I remember right, it was January. It had to be. It was extra cold that week, Stock Show weather. Yeah, it was January. After a short day of work I went home and picked up this book that Joe put in my hands. It was by some kid who lived the life of a hobo. He made it seem romantic but I knew better. The road can crush people. I enjoyed the book anyway, because when I looked up at the clock, it was three in the morning. I needed fresh air. I needed to get off my ass and get my blood pumping. A couple minutes later I hit the street and cruised down the hill towards downtown.

It was a couple degrees above zero when I left my apartment. Steam floated up out of the manhole covers as I coasted on the barren streets. I smiled against the cold and the wind. Tears rolled down my cheeks. I went the wrong way down 17th towards Union Station. I turned around and went back uphill through the 16th Street Mall.

A maintenance truck idled in the middle of the mall with the crew huddling inside. There was one guy unstringing holiday lights from the trees. He looked at me as I passed. I retuned his nod and kept moving.

I turned down the sidewalk before reaching the cluster of hotels near Broadway. I wanted to make one more run before going home.

I jumped the curb and headed downhill again when a cab lurched out of an alley. He missed me only because I managed to swerve off the sidewalk and into the street. I turned to give him the finger, and I think I hit a pothole or a patch of ice. The next thing I knew, my ass was out of the saddle and in the air.

I opened my eyes and the cab driver was talking to me. He was a young white guy no younger than me. Three layers of clothes kept the blacktop from ripping my skin, but my head spun a little when I climbed back on my bike. The cabbie was holding my knit cap in his hands and saying something about wearing a helmet. I grabbed it out of his hands, told him to fuck off, and I rode home.

It felt good to peel my clothes off and get in the shower. The hot water and steam helped to fight off the shivers. Afterwards, I jumped under the covers but could not sleep. My mind kept me awake all night. I stared at the ceiling fan and watched it turn lazy circles.

I've known Stevie a long time. We've been friends almost as long. It's no surprise that our transition from drinking buddies to friends was marked by a woman.

I should start by saying that I was twenty and women were enigmas to me. Still are, really. I've learned how to be comfortable with that. Her mystery was the primary reason I wanted her. Or was it my cluelessness? Either way, I made the mistake of believing that the best way inside her head was through her pussy. A young man's error.

Her name was Emily. She was an art student. Defiant, tomboyish, but shy. She always hung out and could out drink us all. She became even more reclusive when she drank. She would disappear at parties. I never had a moment alone with her. Outside of the typical college bullshit, all we exchanged were glances. Her eyes had a weight to them. They made me feel as if Emily knew more about me than I ever could.

That was especially true on the night of the stupidest thing I've ever done.

(This is the part where I'm supposed to warn you not to do what I did. It's stupid. It's dangerous. You can die. All of this is true. Ultimately, the only person responsible for your stupidity is you)

It was a bet. The details are pure youthful machismo. I won't bore you. The scenario amounted to this: I was supposed to drink a 750ml bottle of Jack Daniels in an hour. What was my reward if I accomplished this feat? A free bottle of Jack Daniels. And if I lost? I would pay for the bottle. Yes, I had more guts than brains.

I broke it down this way: I'd have to drink a shot every minute and a half. That was the only coherent thinking I did that night. Word got around and someone decided that was a good reason to throw a party. It became an event. Dozen's of people would watch some kid drink a bottle of bourbon. Lots of fun.

Here is a list of my only memories from that night:

Before I opened the bottle, someone dragged a huge plastic garbage can over next to me. I thought, oh, that's right. I will be vomiting.

The Talking Head's Stop Making Sense movie was blaring somewhere in another room.

I drank that bottle.

I spent three hours retching into that trash can.

Emily was right there, feeding me water, wiping my face, and keeping me from passing out.

Fast forward a week. I eventually understood how close I came to dying. I walked over to Emily's room and found her door half open. I pushed it open. She was working on something. Big Audio Dynamite was on the boom box and she was furiously rubbing charcoal on a pad of paper. She looked up at me. Her intensity was like a punch in the face.

At that moment, I would have told you that I was in love. I was that kind of fool. The truth was, I wanted the intensity in her eyes. I wanted her creativity. I wanted the strength I saw in her that I could not find inside myself. I was infatuated with, jealous, and covetous of something that I had no idea how to make my own. I was ignorant. All I could see were her hips, tits, and lips.

What do you want Joe?

You're busy, I'll come by later.

Too late, you already interrupted me. Close the door.

She reached over to turn down the music. I caught a flash of her breasts under her shirt. She wasn't wearing a bra.

I just want to say thanks for what you did for me the other night.

Yeah?

Yeah.

And.

Well, I feel like I owe you, but I have no idea how to pay you back.

You want to do something for me?

Yeah, you name it.

Take me out to dinner, a fancy one.

You got it. Any place particular?

Surprise me.

I had no idea if she thought of it that way, but I suddenly had a date with Emily. I started to get hard just thinking about it. I jerked off as soon as I got back to my room.

The date? Typical. Just what you'd imagine if I told you things went well. Did we kiss? We made out during the elevator ride back to her room. When we got to her door she told me to come back tomorrow.

The next day I saw Emily eating lunch with her friends. She watched me watching her. She smirked at me when I showed up at her door later that day.

You almost lost your chance.

I walked in.

I like to take my time.

Do you really?

She closed the door, and pointed me towards the bed.

I sat down like a good boy and enjoyed the show as she undressed. Pink, pink nipples, smooth skin, and strong thighs stood before me. Her straight black hair fell over her shoulders. I stood to undress, and Emily eased me back down on the bed. She pulled my shirt up over my head and left my arms tangled in the sleeves. She brought her face close to mine and her hair swept across my skin. We didn't kiss. She pulled off my jeans and put a blindfold over my eyes. Emily was going to be in charge. That was fine with me.

That's when she took me in her mouth. She didn't leave anything untouched by her tongue. She stepped away for a moment and left me pulsing against the air. She came back and there was the feel of silk on my chest. I recoiled at first, then I relaxed.

Emily ran the silk over me. She wrapped it around the base of my cock and put the rest in her mouth. I knew I would come quick if she kept that up. I reached down and she grabbed the shirt wrapped around my wrists and pushed my hands back.

What do you want?

I want to taste you.

She straddled my chest. Now my arms were pinned under her legs and her pussy was in my face. She went back to work on me. I felt like I was in a race to distract her. She kept moving just past the tip of my tongue. I stretched my neck and buried my nose inside her. I lifted her clit into my mouth with my tongue and held it there. I licked and sucked on that thing like I was trying to save my life. That got Emily's attention. She eased up on me and turned around. I had her in my mouth again and my arms were still pinned. This time I was peeking up at her hard pink nipples from underneath the blindfold.

When she had enough she pulled a condom out and rolled it on me. We fucked slow, came, and collapsed onto each other. When we woke up, it was dark. We ordered Chinese food and lay around naked listening to music.

It was fun like that for a couple weeks. Then she started wanting walk around campus holding hands and talking about meeting her parents. I had to tell Emily that I couldn't be her boyfriend. I just wanted to be friends. She told me that she didn't fuck her friends.

I was sad to lose such a good sex partner. I secretly hoped she was keeping me as her emergency cock under glass. Somehow, I knew we were better off this way. Then came Stevie. About a week after Emily and I stopped seeing each other, Stevie asked me what I thought about him taking her out. I gave him two pieces of advice:

Ask her.

Whatever you do, if you break up with her, don't tell her you just want to be friends.

Three weeks later, what happened? Emily calls me screaming and crying. She called me names and cursed my unborn children. Stevie, without thinking, told her, let's just be friends. I was scumbag number one. With a bullet.

I had to sit Stevie down and give him a lecture about navigating the sometimes rough terrain of female emotions. Like I had any idea. That event seems to have shaped our entire friendship. After ten years, you'd think we'd have something else in common.

She was stumbling out of a windowless bar in New Paltz when I met her.

On the bus from Albany, I convinced the driver to drop me in front of the motel parking lot right off the highway. I dropped my pack in my room and took a walk down Main St. I didn't have a plan beyond stretching my legs and finding a cold beer.

She kept repeating, "You gotta stop them, man. You gotta keep the bastards away from me." She was on something, that much was clear, but I could see she was really afraid and not just being paranoid.

We walked down the sidewalk, and I listened to what she had to say. Her story didn't make a lot of sense. She made three things very clear; she was far from home, she didn't have anywhere to sleep, and someone wanted to hurt her.

She calmed down after a while, and I made an offer.

I've got a room in that motel we passed a couple of blocks back. You can stay with me, no strings.

Will you sleep on the floor?

Sure.

Her head hit the pillow, and she passed out. I realized I didn't even know her name.

I woke up the next morning and her voice was bouncing off the tiles in the shower. It was like the sound of a blue jay in the rain. Her resilience should have been obvious. Later, it would surprise me.

The water stopped, and I listened to her hum as she toweled off.

You awake out there?

Yeah.

So, I'm pretty sure nothing happened last night, but I'm hazy on how we got here.

I stretched out, my feet pushing at the end of my sleeping bag, and let out a low groan.

You were coming out of a bar...

Alone?

Yes, and you were freaking out a little.

Somebody put something in my drink, that much I remember.

We walked and talked for about half an hour.

And you convinced me to come back to your room?

You were coherent...

She got quiet. The bathroom door was closed, and I lay there listening. She started to hum again and it sounded like she was brushing her teeth. I sat up on the floor and gathered the sleeping bag around me.

I'm Stevie.

She stopped brushing.

Hmrhuh?

My name is Stevie.

More brushing, and then spit. It was quiet again and then she opened the door. She stood in the doorway, the bathroom light spilled around her.

Well nice man, most people call me Jackie.

She was wrapped in a motel towel, curly blonde hair down over her shoulders, her bare toes curled on the edge of the carpet.

Thank you.

It felt like we looked at each other like that, she in the door, me on the floor, for a long time. I felt her studying me. Her eyes tested but did not judge. I did the same thing.

When I was a virgin I had a story I would tell girls. It was meant to create an image of a young man who was sexually competent and in possession of some emotional depth. It was my blind attempt at seduction. It was complete bullshit. It went like this:

I lost my virginity when I was 15. I used to spend all my free time at the library. Sometime around the age of twelve I discovered Tolkein and Stephen King. I was hooked. I would go to the library to read and daydream. I was trapped in suburban Long Island and killing time. I noticed one woman who would drop a little girl off for whatever children's program was going on that day. She would then pull a magazine from the shelf and kick off her shoes. I imagined this was the only time she had to herself. She seemed to enjoy it.

She was beautiful in way very specific to Long Island. A salon had almost erased her classic Mediterranean beauty. Almost, but not quite. She was young. At first I thought she was the kid's sister. Maybe her nanny. She certainly looked too young to be a mother. She didn't look like any mom I knew. So, I gathered the courage to talk to her. I had watched plenty of James Bond and John Shaft. I knew how to talk to a woman. She didn't bother to look at me until I said something about her little sister. She shot me a slanted grin and showed me her ring finger. She told me the little girl was her daughter. I stumbled through a complement about how young she looked. She looked at me like I was a joke. I imagined she would enjoy telling the other moms all about me.

As spring turned to summer I would see her more often. I would duck into the stacks until I was sure she was gone. One day I think I was looking for something by Mickey Spillane. She came walking around the corner. She smiled. Her eyes were soft. I saw no indication of judgement. I started to get hard and turned away. She slowed down when she got closer to me. When she passed she turned sideways as if the row was too narrow. Her tits brushed against me. I was the first time in my life that I caught scent of a women's sex. I knew what it was. I knew what it meant. No explanation was necessary.

She was just past kissing distance when she whispered hello over my shoulder. I turned to look at her. Her eyes moved from the swelling in my jeans back up to my eyes.

That's um, quite the situation you've got going on down there.

I was too shocked and embarrassed to speak. I moved my hands to cover myself.

Let me help you with that, okay?

She pressed my hands into my crotch. I squirmed into her touch. I moved my hands away and let her touch me. She rubbed my cock through my jeans. Everything overwhelmed me. In the hushed aisle of a quiet suburban library, I came for the first time from a woman's touch. It felt like I had exploded. She put her fingers against my lips to remind me to keep quiet. I never imagined anything like it. I stood deep in the stacks quivering. She kissed my cheek and walked away.

See ya.

I spent all day in that row of books. I waited for my jeans to dry and tried to comprehend what just happened.

A week later, I was reading a magazine and she pulled up a chair next to me.

Hi.

Uh, hello.

Look, don't be embarrassed.

I'm not, just a little surprised. I thought you were married.

What's your name?

Joe.

Pleased to meet you, you can call me Sara. We shook hands.

How old are you Joe?

Seventeen.

I lied. She sat looking at me.

I lied again.

Okay, sixteen. How old are you?

Well, that's not too bad. I'm only 23, so it's not completely cradle snatching.

I don't know if she really was 23. She looked like she could be younger than that.

Look, I am married. So don't start getting any wild fantasies in your head. My daughter is the best thing to ever happen to me, and right now she can have all the things I never had growing up. I'm not going to ruin that for her just because of you, right?

Sure.

If you can be a grown up about this, we can have a little fun, and I can teach you something. Okay?

I looked at her. Was my virginity that obvious?

Clock's ticking Joe…speak up. You won't get this kind of chance again.

Yes.

Meet me in the elevator in fifteen minutes.

We spent the next two weeks making out. I kept pushing. Up her shirt, down her pants. She would stop me, put my hands in my pockets, and start kissing me again. I was confused. I realize now that she was breaking me like a wild animal. We made out wherever we could find a private corner. When I got to the point where I could kiss her for fifteen minutes without creaming myself, she moved things to the back seat of her car.

There was a tree in the corner of the library parking lot. We spent that summer parked under it's shade. I explored her body in the back of her minivan. I was introduced to the mystery of the clitoris. I learned the difference between a strong hand and a stiff hand. I stumbled through cunnilingus. By the time we actually had sex, I couldn't get enough. I think we only ended up fucking because she was bored. She dumped me the next week. It was over.

The week before school started I was in the mall shopping for clothes. I saw Sara with her daughter and husband. I watched them walk past the store I was in. He was carrying the little girl on his shoulders. Sara spotted me. She looked right through me. She didn't even blink.

If you know anything about 17, 18, 19 year old girls, you already know this story had a zero percent success rate. I would've had better luck admitting I was a virgin. But that's not the point. The point is, although it would be another 10 years before I started writing, this was the first story I ever told.

I slept three nights on the floor of that motel room until Jackie finally let me up on the bed. Then, she made me slept under the sheets while she slept under the bedspread. We hung out, walked around New Paltz some, but mostly we flipped around the cable channels trying to avoid pictures of the war. It was okay.

Over the course of a week she told me her story. She was on the run from her husband. He was dealing meth and had started using it. She was afraid things were going to get worse, so she left. He was somewhere in North Carolina. She didn't think he would come after her, but she wanted to keep low until she felt safe.

I still had questions, but I didn't bother asking. I didn't care about her past, I just wanted to spend some time in this quiet little thing we had fallen into.

I was laying in bed thinking about things and listening to her brush her teeth. When she got into bed, she slid under the sheets with me. I looked at her naked body. Jackie was athletic and strong, she had the body of a dancer. Our hands reached out, and we pulled each other close. She touched my face and we kissed. She opened her mouth to me and I could feel her breathing. Nothing else mattered at that moment.

I bent down and took her nipple in my mouth. It was like a pebble on my tongue. Circle, circle, tug, and lick, she pushed my head to her other breast. I reached down and cupped her ass in my hands. Her soft skin fit perfect in my palms. She rolled over to her other side and pressed into me. I kissed the back of her neck and buried my face in her curls. My fingers found her mouth. My other hand opened her lips and dipped inside her. I could feel the hum of her body in my fingertips.

She pressed deeper into me, reaching down for me between her legs. She put me inside of her and slid over me. I scooped my arm under her and lifted her. I rolled to my back, keeping her on top of me. She was on auto pilot, moving without thinking, and I just let it happen. She arched her back, and the top of her head was under my chin. She was wrapped around me from tip to base. I caressed her body from below and behind.

I'm coming.

Jackie let herself go, I pulled out and came on her thighs and stomach.

She lay on top of me gulping air.

You wanna drink?

Yes, she exhaled.

Damn. I feel like a five-dollar whore during Mardi Gras. My balls are sore. My back feels like it's about to start cramping up. I'm walking down Colfax on a Sunday morning because the damn 15 bus is not on schedule. Again. I spent last night with some schoolteacher. Sister rode me like a rocking horse all night long. Then she kicked me out. That's me, Joe the cockhorse.

This shit has got to stop.

My 16-year-old self would kick my ass for complaining about having too much sex. He would laugh at the idea. I was a kid who'd masturbate all afternoon and then pass out with dried come caked on my stomach. Every other week I thought he was in love with a different girl. I was happy just to dry hump a girl's leg. I had no idea.

If I'm supposed to be such a grown up, why am I living a teenager's fantasy? It's true, adulthood is wasted on adults...and I'm regressing.

Damn.

What kind of dog are you?

Where the fuck is this coming from Stevie?

That keeps popping into my head whenever I get into elevators lately. I watch the other people standing there, fidgeting, acting nervous, making friendly conversation, dominating their space, cowering, whatever, and all I can think to myself is "what kind of dog are you?"

Oh, I gotta hear all about this. Tell me more.

This is not some exercise in polite dinner conversation, I mean it. If your mental and emotional characteristics were somehow translated into canine form, what would that be?

What does that have to do with elevators?

I think the enclosed space makes people exaggerate themselves. If they're driven by fear, they get more afraid, if they're pushy, aggressive people, they get even more so. You see?

Maybe. So, what kind of dog are you?

The way things are going lately, I feel like a poorly fed Great Dane.

Are you drunk?

Not yet. Buy the next round.

So Stevie wanted to audition for one those television dating shows. What a nimrod. He asked me to help him shoot his audition tape. Why not, I figured. At least I'll get to watch him make an ass of himself.

So I dug out my video camera and tripod and set them up in the living room. He plopped down on the couch and started talking to the camera. He sounded silly and desperate. There was no way I would let him send that tape out. I offered to play it back for him and hoped he'd see what I saw. I didn't count on what happened next.

I rewound to the head of the tape and pushed play. On the screen there was a brief flicker, two seconds tops, of me in my full bare ass nakedness fucking an old girlfriend doggie style. By the time I reach over and shut off the television, it was too late. The image had neatly cleaved our friendship into before and after that moment.

I did not need to see that.

All I could do was laugh uncontrollably.

Augh, there is no way I'm going to be able to wipe that image out of my brain.

I was wiping tears from my eyes.

What the hell were you two thinking? Did she know about this?

Oh man, absolutely. It was her idea.

And she let you keep the tape after you broke up?

I told her I erased it.

I can't believe it. You have no boundaries, do you?

I forgot I had it. There's a lot more...

I've seen more of your naked ass than I ever want to see again. If I see any more, I may have to stop being your friend. Please destroy that tape.

And that was the last time he mentioned being on a reality dating show.

I sat with Jackie in the back row of New Paltz's movie theatre watching another dumb comic book action movie. We had to get out of that motel room. It was the middle of the day and the movie theater was empty except for the old couple three or four rows in front of us. I looked over at Jackie. Actually, she caught me while I looked at her tits. She smiled her smile. I reached over and we started making out.

She didn't hesitate; she reached into my jeans and took hold of me. I buried my face into her neck and nibbled on her shoulder. She put her mouth near my ear and whispered.

Don't get us thrown out of here.

To hell with them, I want you.

I moved my hand into her hair and nudged her down. She looked in my eyes and smiled again as she dropped between my legs.

She cupped me in her hand and gently kissed. I reached down and moved her hair from her face as she began to work her tongue around me. Just before she took me in her mouth I could feel her breath hot on me. I took my hand away, and she looked up at me. Jackie shook her head and put my hand back on her head. I was too busy enjoying myself to be surprised.

She moved her mouth over me, stopping only to swirl an occasional circle, or to hold all of me in her mouth. Jackie was good. She didn't need any guidance from me. I closed my eyes as I could feel my toes start to tighten. I wanted to come. The movie's end credits started to roll and rock music blared in the dark. She wrapped her hand around me and pumped.

Jackie...

I opened my eyes and the old woman was standing in the aisle looking at us. I couldn't hear her, but I watched her mouth move as she recoiled.

I can't believe this!

I released into Jackie's mouth and looked into her lifted eyes. They were glittering with pleasure. We smiled at each other in the dark. Fuck 'em, I thought, they wish they had it this good.

On the way back to the motel we picked up a bottle of bourbon and talked; about getting old, the war, good movies. It was one of those stupid conversations you have when you think you're in love.

There were three sick ass Harleys in the motel parking lot. Not the brand new, off the showroom, yuppie kind, but choppers. These were real road hogs. They had been chopped for speed and didn't have any gauges or excessive chrome. One of them looked like it was made from parts of three different generations of Harley motorcycle. The heat from a long day's ride was still coming off the engines. Enthralled with those damned bikes, I didn't even turn to look at Jackie when she told me she was going to get us some ice and soda. That would have been my last look at her.

The room was dark when I opened the door. Before I turned on the light, something hard crashed against the back of my head. Someone turned on the lights and all I saw were three shadows. Three huge motherfuckers.

Where is she?

One of them stretched out some duct tape and covered my mouth. A heavy boot stepped on my hand, crushing it into the cheap carpet. Something in my pinkie snapped.

I'm going to ask one more time. Where is she?

This was her husband and his friends, Jackie had figured that out in the parking lot. She ran off and let me walk into that room alone. She was a smart girl. I started to understand what was going on.

Before I made a sound, someone kicked me in the ribs. You see it in the movies all the time and it looks what it is, a stunt. You can't imagine the tremendous pain that a two hundred some odd pound man in steel toe boots can inflict. I screamed into the tape and shook my head. The boot slammed into my ribcage again. Either they didn't understand that I wanted to talk, or didn't care. That's when the beating really began. They pummeled the shit out of me. I think the only reason they stopped to take the tape off my mouth was to listen to me beg. I took a deep breath and I almost choked on my own blood. I decided to try to buy her some time.

I know where her money is.

Fuck that, where is she?

This time the boot connected to my chin. I felt my teeth rattle in my jaw. I think I blacked out. Through gray consciousness I heard them talking.

Let's just get the money. Fuck it man, she's gone.

Someone rolled me over, propped me against the bed, and handed me a wet washcloth. I coughed up a huge ball of bloody phlegm and spat it on the floor.

Where's the money?

I inhaled again and there wasn't any blood. I lifted my head and for the first time, I saw my attackers. I looked them over, and the thought occurred to me that I might end up dying in that motel room. There was a little guy, well, he was smaller than the other two. He had a braided beard and a bandana over his head. A ponytail ran down his back and his bandana was flopping around loose on his head. He looked like he had just finished handing out an ass kicking. I think that was Mr. Boot. The one crouched in front of me was older, and he had a shaved head. The third guy looked clean cut, except for the words white devil tattooed across the front of his neck. If he was in a suit, you would have thought he was a college jock going to his first job interview.

I pointed to the bedside table. The kid went over and opened the drawer. He pulled out the King James and shook it open.

Hey idiot, you're not gonna find fifty grand in a bible.

I had no idea Jackie was carrying that kind of money. I fully understood how fucked up things were. The bald guy turned to me. His scalp, not shaved I noticed, just bald, furrowed into deep crevices when he looked at me. He pointed two fingers on one of his huge hands at me. His eyes hardened. He spoke one word and he made it clear that the right answer would keep me alive.

Where?

My jaw felt like it was about to fall off my skull, so I lifted my good hand and turned my palm over. I hoped with to God he understood. It took a second, but he got it.

Pull the drawer out and turn it over.

And there it was, my thousand dollar bankroll, stuffed into a plastic sandwich bag and taped to the bottom of the drawer. I prayed.

Mr. Boot stepped over and snatched the bag from the kid. He didn't need to look at it for long. He came over, pushed the bald guy out of his way and squatted down to look me right in my face. He pulled a folding knife out of his belt and opened it. He pressed the point under my eye.

Enough bullshit. Where is Jackie, and where is my money?

Ah dun gnow.

I shook my head the tiniest bit, and a tear ran down my cheek.

He pressed a little harder, and the tip of the blade broke through my skin. I told the only truth I knew.

Gohn. Shre leht. Ah dun gnow.

The man was angry and ready to quit. Now this was just a problem that needed cleaning up. He pulled the knife away from my face and I could see him trying to decide what to do. I couldn't believe Jackie fucked with this guy. How stupid. That was my last conscious thought before he punched me in the face and knocked me out.

When I woke up, my head was leaning on air-conditioned glass. This was a bus. My left hand was in a makeshift splint, my torso was wrapped in bandages underneath my clothes, and there was a bottle of ibuprofen in my jacket pocket. There was a ticket envelope on the inside pocket. In it was a ticket to Scranton, $500, and a note from Jackie.

I didn't bother reading it. I just put my head back on the glass. It felt good as I watched the traffic pass.

There was a dog standing in the oncoming traffic lane. It was staring down the truck that was about to run it over.

I thought, that's me.

Life became significantly more interesting when Emily invited me to visit her in Los Angeles.

It was January, Stock Show season, a perfect moment to get out of Denver. A string of cold nights found me hunkered down at home making blind attempts to write. After a couple of scotches the page was still blank. After five nights of nothing, I picked up the phone and drunk dialed Emily.

Hey Joe, what's going on?

New year, same war.

Quiet night night at home?

Too quiet.

Yeah, we kept in touch. She eventually got over what happened and we became close. It helped that she moved to Los Angeles after she graduated. Oh, I still had crush on her those first few years. It was tough. I got to hear all about her trials as a hot single woman in L.A. Part of me believes she knew she was torturing me. My only solace was knowing that most of her dates turned out to be gay men. For a while, we were the only significant members of the opposite sex in each other's lives. I learned a lot about how to listen to a woman.

What, no lady to keep you warm?

These Denver women are all scenesters or suburban mom wannabes.

She giggled. I was tired of talking about myself.

Life treating you well Em?

I'm between projects now so things are slow.

She left Denver years ago and found work in architectural design. She once told me about a client flipping out because the knob on the door to his strip mall store was too small. Knobs, what a racket.

Listen to the two of us. Are we getting old or what?

There was silence. I pulled the phone from my ear to check the signal.

Did you hear me Joe?

What?

I said, what are you doing next week?

Same ol' bullshit.

After a while I just stopped wanting her. The distance had something to do with it. I eventually came to think of her as a friend. To be honest, she was my first female friend. There's only one good way to sum up how the situation evolved: sex you can have right now is always better than sex you have to wait for. Crude, but true.

I've got some vacation time to burn, why don't you come out for a couple of days?

It was my turn to be quiet, but not too long. My hesitation would prompt Emily to take the offer back as quick as she threw it at me.

Sure, what else have I got to do.

I made travel arrangements. She scheduled the time off. She made an offer of an air mattress. I told her I wouldn't impose on her like that. She insisted. I said we'll see.

A week later I was on a westbound train. It's my favorite way to travel. I could lie and tell you that I like trains because they're romantic. Fact is, if you're not traveling in a sleeper car it's not much different than taking the bus. That's Stevie mode of travel. He likes to keep it blue collar. I like the train because it's slow. There's plenty of time and space to fill. These things are valuable to someone who thinks he's a writer.

When I got off the train all I wanted was a hot shower and a cold beer. Emily was at the station waiting for me. She looked sharp dressed up for work. She was still in great shape. Shit, she was in better shape than when we were in college. She had no problem showing it off either. She may have been at some junior level at her firm, but she wasn't wearing junk off the rack. Her suit was tailored and she had on some kind of silk top under her jacket. She filled her jacket in that unmistakable way when a woman knows her breasts are the equivalent of broad shoulders on a man. It's an expression of power.

She never needed to put in a lot of effort. Emily's family is from South America. Her beauty is a combination of the indigenous mountain people and their Castilian conquerors. She's got full lips, a gracefully curved nose, heavy eyelids, and long lashes that cover sharp hazel eyes. All of this is crowned by hair like black satin that falls to her shoulders. The whole package is dangerous. The real impact is finding out that Emily's soft features camouflage a relentless spirit.

I tried to think nothing of it when she kissed me hello. She lingered on my lips just a little. My body flushed and my heart roared in my ears. Walking to her car, I reminded myself that I was in Los Angeles. The customs are different here. My policy is it's always better to assume nothing. At the same time, I started putting together a list of indirect questions to figure out what was going on in her sex life. Before she could put her car in reverse, she beat me to it.

How are the ladies treating you Joe?

My current dry streak felt like I was throwing pennies down an empty well too many times. I was trying to keep things casual at the moment. Being gainfully unemployed is hard work. Especially when you're a functional drunk. Even a casual relationship tilts everything out of balance. I told Emily a meaningless lie.

It's been better, but I can't complain.

She laughed and I let my tension go. My standard temperament is to carry my emotions like a clenched fist waiting to strike. Or be pried open. When she smiled at me, it's like a sunshine ice pick. It didn't matter if we fucked. It didn't matter if we didn't. Her laugh and her smile completely disarm me. Still. I started thinking about a cold shower.

Yeah, me neither.

I thought that would be the end of the sexual strain between us. I needed it to be. I had decided to stay at her place. If things went poorly I could end up sleeping in a park somewhere. We stopped on the way to her place so she could show me some of her work. It was another mall. She was not pleased when I said that.

It's a retail resort.

Oookay.

Really, this is way beyond your standard issue big box mall. We studied all the major shopping destinations in the western world and distilled them down to create an experience. Every detail here has been thought through. Right down to the height of the curbs.

I looked at her.

When did you start drinking the Kool-Aid?

Seriously, Joe, I'm really proud of my work here.

Okay, show me.

She took me into the baroque movie theater lobby. She showed me the million dollar staircase in the computer store. She made me stand in front of the dancing waters. I kept my mouth shut until the theme park trolley loaded with tourists rolled by.

Cute. When do we start drinking?

Emily rolled her eyes. It was hard not telling her how disappointed I was. This is what she would have to show for her talent when she dies. She could see that I had my fill. We went to a restaurant a couple of blocks away. We sat at a table on the sidewalk. Someone brought us menus and Emily left the table.

She came back with a bottle of Rioja from the wine shop next to the restaurant. She stood it on the table like a challenge.

We're going to need more than that.

She laughed.

I'm not kidding. I drink at altitude. It takes twice as much to make a dent in me down here at sea level.

Pace yourself champ. There's no rush.

The place served tapas. After four or five small plates, and a bucket of clams, we opened a second bottle. I was ready to really talk.

What happened to you?

What?

When was the last time you painted?

She sat looking at me.

I know you like your job, and you have to do something to make a living, but shit, is that it?

I waved a hand in the direction of the, ahem, retail resort.

For a moment the old intensity was back in her eyes. She did not look happy to have me for company.

It must be easy for you to sit there and judge me. You've got-

I'm not judging you-

-money to live on and time to wander around and write as you see fit.

-I just hate to see you wasting yourself on something so trivial.

She looked at me again. It was as if she just realized the color of my eyes. She reached out and poured the last of the bottle into our glasses.

Joe, we're going to sit here and finish our wine. If you manage to not piss me off, we can keep having a good time. I'm just going to say one thing, and then our conversation about this will end.

Emily lowered her chin and looked at me from the corner of her eyes. I recognized this particular piece of drunken body language. This is what she does when she's digging in and will not be budged.

You understand me?

I lifted my glass and took a sip in acknowledgment.

What I do matters. You might not think it's all that creative, and you're right, a hundred years from now none of it will mean anything. Us grown ups have to make our way through the world as best we can, and I don't have to justify myself, or what I do for a living, to anyone. Don't push me. Don't make me regret inviting you to see me.

I raised my glass again.

To today.

Today.

We emptied our glasses.

It didn't take long to go from there to her bedroom. That's typical for us. We never rush, we never hesitate. As usual, I was the last to know.

She didn't live far from the restaurant. I watched the scenery roll past the passenger window as Emily drove. It was dark. Everything looked like a strip mall. Other than the occasional palm tree it didn't look any different from the rest of America. I realized that my weariness was affecting my attitude. I promised myself to give L.A. another chance to impress me after a long shower and a good night's rest.

We walked into her place and I dropped my bag next to the couch. I sat on the couch and immediately started looking around for a television remote. No luck. She locked the front door and went upstairs. I listened to her close the bathroom door, brush her teeth, flush the toilet, and leave the bathroom. Her footfalls moved across the ceiling followed by the sound of her bedroom door closing. I slumped on Emily's couch. An air mattress sat unfilled in a corner of the room. I gave up on finding a remote. I listened to her footsteps on the floor over my head. Then the place fell quiet.

After a few minutes I pushed off the couch. I climbed to the top of the steps and went into the bathroom. Emily had left towels out for me. I slid the shower door open and started the water. I adjusted the temperature to just above lukewarm and I stepped in. I stood there. The water fell over me, useless. I couldn't feel it. I didn't want to. I picked up the soap and washed myself without thinking.

Too numb to be shocked, I just stared when Emily walked in. I looked through the glass at her. She looked back at me and grinned a little while taking off her robe. She stood before me and let my eyes ramble over her body. I opened the shower door and offered her my hand. She took it and stepped into the water. She immediately gave the hot water knob a firm twist.

She moved in close. I wrapped my arms around her. She rested her head under my chin. The water fell over and around us. We washed each other. She scrubbed my back. I washed her hair. My hands found the curve of Emily's hips. She still felt familiar. She tilted her face to mine and we kissed. My cock began to rise. She stepped back and rinsed off. After she got out, I rinsed the soap off my body and shut the water.

She let her towel fall to the floor and handed me another. Emily watched me dry myself. Her face revealed her usual combination of curiosity and direct observation. She walked out and turned down the hallway. I took a moment to glance in the mirror. I looked for, and found no trace of, doubt. I was done thinking for the night. I followed Emily's naked body into her bedroom.

She lay on her back across the length of the bed with one knee cocked in the air and her other leg hanging over the side of the bed. I stood over Emily's body. I enjoyed the view. She propped herself on her elbows and placed the sole of her foot on my chest.

If I remember right, you're not afraid of pussy.

I could hear the smile in Emily's voice. I picked her foot up and moved in between her legs. Her thighs were cool and smooth against my cheeks. I teased her with licks and kisses everywhere but where she wanted. Her cilt was hard.

I got the impression that no one had ever properly given Emily head. I stopped teasing her and got down to business. She couldn't get enough. She had her thighs wrapped around my ears and her muffled voice barely registered.

She pushed me off. We both caught our breath. She pointed to a dark wooden box on her nightstand. It was filled with a jumble of condoms. I pulled open one of the packets. I turned back and Emily was on her stomach with her ass in the air.

Joe, you're the only man I trust enough to treat me like a pig.

She wiggled it at me. That was all I needed. I rolled the condom on and knelt on the bed between her knees. I started slow and made sure to feel every inch of her. She was firm in my hands. It was familiar, yet still, the thrill of new sensation connected us. Emily moved in time with each stroke. The deeper I went, the higher I climbed on top of her, until I was up on my feet and crouched above her. I pulled at her hips. She let me push and pull her back and forth.

Joe the pig fucker, that's me.

I came, pulled out, and collapsed on the bed. I didn't have time to start feeling bad about treating her so rough. Emily squirmed over to my chest and caressed my face. Her face had a sweaty shine. Her wet hair draped across her cheeks. Damn. I've never known anyone who could be so strong and so vulnerable at the same time. What an amazing woman.

I woke up the next morning to the smell of fresh coffee. There was a cup on the nightstand. There was a folded note propped next to it. I picked up the note and walked to the bathroom. Emily's heels clipped against the tiled floor downstairs. The front door closed. I lifted the toilet seat and streamed into the bowl. I pushed the curtain aside on the window above the toilet and watched Emily walk across the street. She got into her car and drove off. I unfolded and read her note.

Joe,

I had a fun last night. I hope you did too. But please don't think you owe me some kind of romantic gesture. You're friendship is very important to me, and really, it's the only thing we owe each other. Let's not confuse things. I don't need any friends with benefits right now. Please. I think we're better off just forgetting about it. Otherwise, we might just end up in a real relationship. And I'm not sure either of us can deal with that. Help yourself to whatever, I left the spare key next to the coffee machine.

Em.

I watched Emily go off into her day. I thought about how long it had been since I felt like I could leave giant footsteps on the world. I thought about how long it had been since I felt my heart pound with passion for any reason. I'm not big on the idea of muses. All that waiting for divine inspiration can make a man lazy. It had been a long time since I wanted to stand against all those things in the world that can tear a man down. I read Emily's note again. I looked back out the window. A rat scurried down a palm tree silhouetted against a vague blue sky. Emily is capable of more real soul than the world deserves. Fuck it, I thought. The world can go to hell, but I can't let this woman get away.

I am the man with the gun. Let's not forget that.

Laura says nothing, but her eyes sneer at me. I don't really want to shoot this guy, but my wife was just snorting coke off his cock. The man needs a lesson.

I should have seen this coming; I'm out on the road all the time. At best, I might see her one weekend a month. She's got no job, doesn't go to school, there's nothing going on for her outside of scheduling my trips and watching the money pile up in the bank. Should I have expected anything else?

She shoves him off the couch, cursing and kicking at him as he falls. He's trying to talk his way out of this and she's furious. I don't feel any better knowing I've been on the receiving end of her temper once or twice.

You should shoot him just for being such a punk.

Fucking bitch!

Both of you calm the fuck down. Getting jumpy will only get someone hurt.

The guy lays there, his eyes bouncing back and forth between the gun and his pants. He can't decide to bolt or make a grab for the gun. I can see it in his eyes. Laura stands naked, clenching her fists, and seething. If I don't rein both of them in right quick, I could lose control here.

You, get your pants on. Laura, pack a bag and call a cab.

She steps over him, making a move towards me.

You don't mean that.

I step back and point the gun in her direction. She freezes.

We're done. Just sit down and relax while your friend here gets dressed.

She does what I tell her, but I know she's already calculating her next move.

Dude, I had no idea. She told me you were dead.

Shut up!

She kicks him again.

If you listen to her and get dressed, you might get out of here alive.

He gets up on his knees and moves away from Laura. Keeping an eye on me, his hand searches for, and finds, his pants. Laura can barely contain herself.

This is your fault, you know. I wouldn't have to lower myself with this trash if you were doing right by me.

And how could I do that, huh? You won't go on the road with me, you won't get a job, all you do is party and sit around the house.

Fuck you, you knew what I was all about when you married me.

You're right, I should've known better. Now I do.

The guy buckles his belt and is backing towards the door.

You're both nuts.

And he's out the door.

I pull the cell phone from the clip on my belt and thumb the number for a cab. I watch Laura scowl at me beyond the barrel of the pistol. The dispatcher picks up the line and I give our address. I hang up.

Grab a bag, take what you can carry. You're leaving.

She opens her mouth, but says nothing. Her eyes move from the gun in my hand to my eyes. I keep my mouth shut. I watch her throw some clothes and make up in a gym bag. She puts on a pair of jeans and her favorite black boots.

If I don't get an address from you in a week, the rest of your stuff will be on the sidewalk.

She walks to the door and turns to me.

Pete...

Now come the tears. Not a full flow, mind you, just a touch of wetness in the corners of her eyes. She can't even commit to bullshitting me. She's done this so many times, she should know I can see right through her.

One last kiss?

She steps closer, both hands holding the bag behind her back. I don't move towards her, but I lower the gun and let her lay her head on my chest. I can smell the smoke in her hair. She kisses my collarbone, and nibbles her way up my neck. She moves to my lips and I turn my head away.

The corner of my eye catches the flash of the bag just before I am clocked in the head. Her knee sends a blast of pain through my nuts and up my spine. I'm on my knees. Laura kicks me across the face, and bends down, picking up the pistol. The last thing I see before I blackout is her ass shaking out the door.

It had been two weeks since I slept in my own bed. I shuffled into a windowless bar in Cleveland hoping to get a shot of bourbon and pass out in a dark corner.

There were two guys on stools underneath a silent television. They were ignoring the pictures of tanks and soldiers rolling across the screen. The bottle of tequila sitting on the bar in front of them didn't have much life left in it.

The bartender didn't say anything, he just stood there looking at me. I suppose he was trying to decide if he was going to throw me out. I pulled five dollars out of my pocket.

Bourbon.

He reached down into the rack and pulled out the bottle. The other hand produced a dull, scratched, shot glass. The three second pour felt generous until I lifted the glass and my nose told me right away that the booze had been watered down. I shot the bastard a weak glance and carried my drink to the furthest booth I could see.

I set the glass in front of me and sank onto the smoky worn wooden bench. I closed my eyes and let the voices of the two men sitting at the bar tumble over me.

There was this woman in Sioux Falls.

Yeah?

Best blow job ever.

Really?

Shaft, balls, head, she worked the whole unit. A real pro.

Did she swallow?

Are you listening to me? This was not some sorority girl you pick up at a kegger. This woman was not afraid of dick. It would have been an insult to tell her when I was coming. She knew it was happening before I did.

Blow jobs. Heh. Right on cue, out of nothing but memory, she slid into the booth with me. I thought I had left her back in New Paltz.

How's it hangin' Stevie?

A little to the left.

She hung her face over my drink and wrinkled her nose at it.

Some things never change huh. Still drinking this shite?

Jackie's curls were pulled back from her face, held in place by a tortoise shell comb. Her cheeks were still a little girl's cheeks, and her short nose was faintly dotted with freckles. Her eyes were what gave her away. The shine in her eyes stripped away the freshness from her all American face. When I first saw her hard, bright, eyes, I knew I would fall in love with Jackie.

What are you doing here?

You can't cut me loose. Even if you wanted to.

Well, there's a lot to forget.

I know, I can't believe how much life we squeezed into a couple of weeks.

What were we thinking? How dare we believe that passion could fuel us forever? Were we fools? Naive? Blinded by the physical chemistry of our lust?

Of course I didn't say those things. I just sat with the memory of her, and held myself tight.

Stevie, you, and men like you will be obsolete in a hundred years.

Joe's been ranting for almost a half hour. Mostly he's been going off on his favorite piñata, technology. This last comment took me by surprise. I take a pull from my beer and ask him to repeat himself.

You heard me.

Okay, I'll bite. Why should I care about how useful I'll be in a hundred years?

Let me put it to you in the form of a question; what do you have to offer a that can't be replaced by a machine?

Oh. Well, thank God I won't be around long enough to deal with that.

Won't you? How old are you, thirty?

Don't rush it, I'm twenty-eight.

Assuming you don't start smoking, or drink yourself into the ground, with the continued march of science and medicine, you've got at least another eighty years left on this spinning ball of mud.

Joe raises his glass to toast this piece of information and watches me while he drains his drink. I never gave it much thought, but I can see that he's right. I finish my drink and wait for him to make his point.

God forbid your gene pool should be allowed to continue, but let's just say you manage to reproduce. On the happy day your five or six year old drops the birds and bees question in your lap, what could you possibly say that isn't already outdated as we sit here waiting to order our next round? How do you prepare a child to live in a world you can't imagine? Just how old do you think you'll be on that momentous occasion?

My recent string of romantic disasters, especially New Paltz, has pretty much put me off even speaking to women, much less think about having a family. But I know that I'll bounce back, so, anything is possible. Joe looks at me, waiting for an answer.

You're assuming a lot.

How about this, I'll answer the original question for you and buy the next round.

Who am I to say no?

First, you've got the one thing that no pill, petri dish, or packet of computer code can replace: human compassion. Second, you're a man of intellect. With study and application, you could move beyond relying on your back and your legs to make a living. You're young. If you do the work, in ten years or so you might be ready to face that new world. At the very least you'll have something of substance to offer anyone insane enough to get entangled with you. The only real question is whether you have the will.

For what?

To do the work.

What about you? Have you done the work?

Let's step up from the suds shall we, something stronger? I'm having Irish whiskey. What are you drinking?

The dream came to me again last night. This time when I opened my mouth, it was filled with sharp shards of glass. I couldn't move my lips or tongue for fear of shredding them.

Again, there were no sweaty sheets, no heaving screams. There was only the sound of traffic outside my window. And me, in the dark, alone.

I threw the covers back, dressed, and went out for a run. When I got back I threw a load of clothes in the washing machine, sat down at my kitchen table, and read some Louis L'amour. By the time the sun came up, I had a pot of coffee in me and was ready for work. I'm on the streets for twelve mind and ass numbing hours, driving a cab.

So I picked up a fare at a downtown hotel, and he started with the questions. For some reason, people think cabbies, bartenders, and prostitutes have to be great conversationalists. Everyday there's at least one. They want to talk about the weather, they want to talk sports, they want to talk about themselves.

Mostly, they want to suck the life out of you. Maybe they're nervous or bored. Maybe they're drunk. Maybe they are sincerely interested in your life. I say bullshit. I think it just makes them feel better about their own lives, "thank god I'm not that poor sucker", that kind of shit. It's not enough to be tourists in their own lives, they want to take a little vacation in yours.

I take people where they're going and I keep my mouth shut. I get paid to drive. If I have to, I give them grunts and single syllable answers. Most people get the message and leave me alone, but not today. Not this fucker. He wouldn't let it go. So I gave him the encapsulated version:

It pays the bills.

Yes, I'm a student.

Grad school.

Civil engineering.

I run triathlons.

Then he launches into how much of an athlete he used to be. People are so self absorbed. On top of all that, he shorted me on the tip. That's how the rest of my shift went. Man, I hate people. So, nine o'clock rolls around, and I was ready to make my last run of the night. I pulled up to the address the dispatcher gave me and a woman slid in. I asked where she wanted to go.

Hold on a sec.

I turned around and the barrel of a gun was pointed at my face. My jaw dropped open, my lips parted to speak. I heard the sound of the hammer click back and I thought it was over.

Shut up, give me your money, and take me to the airport.

I did what she said, too many people get killed trying to be heroes. I handed over nearly a month's rent without looking back. At the airport, she left the gun in the back seat. I figure it was a fair trade. I'll just have to work another shift.

The sign above the counter read, PLEASE DO NOT HELP YOURSELF. The cover of the menu was a crudely drawn deer underneath the words El Bambi. I fell asleep on the bus before it left Vegas city limits, and when I found myself waking up at a rest stop lunch counter, with my new girlfriend flirting with the locals, I wondered what new level of hell this place was and hoped it wouldn't include eating roadkill.

The fun started when she walked back from the bathroom and sat on the stool next to me. The three teenagers in the booth behind us started talking to her. They told her they knew what she needed, they told her they had what she needed, they told her that all she had to do was get up and sit with them. They used words like coochie and tube steak. They were polite fellows.

I thought, well, my ass has been kicked because of a woman once already this year, the odds were pretty good that I could stomp these kids. When I turned to face the boys, she put her hand on my shoulder and spoke to them.

You really think you can handle all this?

She held her coat open. They could see her clinging t-shirt. They looked at how her legs stretched up into a pair of shorts that stopped a few inches short of hooker. The boys had nothing to say. That is, until she turned away from them.

Com'ere bitch, I'll give something you won't forget.

That's when I stood up.

Later, in the parking lot, I lay in the dirt and spat blood. An old mexican man was leaning over me.

Are you okay my friend?

Where am I?

This was my introduction to Beaver, Utah.

I met Laura in Vegas. In the forty eight hours leading up to this humiliation at the rest stop, she shanghaied me to join her celebration bender. The occasion? She told me her husband was dead.

She had a room at Caesar's. When we weren't drinking or fucking, or drinking and fucking, we spent her money in the casino. Sunday came and it was time for me to leave. She bought a bus ticket to go back to Denver with me. It felt like a good idea.

The old man helped me back on the bus and the kids scurried off before the local law showed up. Laura was back in her seat. The old man dropped me in the chair next to her and muttered something as he walked off.

Putana Diablo...

That was all I heard. Laura reached over and brushed my hair off my face. A woman like this was new to me. She was more of a woman than most of the girls I wasted my time with. It wasn't because she was older. It wasn't because wore my ass out in bed. There was something about the way she treated me. It was as if she didn't need me, but she wanted me anyway.

Are you okay baby?

Oh yeah, all roses and candy.

That was very impressive. That was a first.

What, no one's ever defended your honor?

What, my honor? Sweet Stevie. No, no one's ever gotten their ass kicked for me.

She started kissing and cooing all over me. Even with a bloody nose and a scrape on my cheek, I don't need mothering. Somehow, her attention made me feel better.

What are you talking about, ass kicked, I held my own until that third kid jumped in.

How old do think the were? Sixteen?

I don't know, didn't you ask them?

Her reply was silence and a glare. The kissing and stroking stopped. Just as well, the bus driver was making his way up the aisle.

Am I going to have to leave you two here?

She crossed her arms and turned towards her reflection in the window. I gave the driver my best apologetic look.

No, I'm sure we can manage to behave ourselves till we get to Denver.

Make sure you do. I don't have any problem leaving you by the side of the road.

He looked over at her and back to me. His glance seemed to ask, buddy, do you have any idea what you're doing?

Thanks.

He didn't acknowledge me, he just turned and walked back. Laura turned back to me.

He might be doing you a favor. Maybe this was a mistake.

I let her words sit between us and I wondered if there was any truth in them.

The bus engine blasted alive. The driver turned off the interior lights and steered back to the highway. We were northbound in the Utah desert night.

Laura took off her dungaree jacket off, spread it over herself, and assumed the posture of sleep. Her silence was supposed to be my punishment. So be it, I thought I could do without all the attitude.

I didn't sleep. The bus glided through the canyons. The sky was clear but the stars were blocked out by the high canyon walls. The only light came from the half moon as it moved from one side of the bus to the other as we negotiated the twisting road. I glimpsed Laura's legs in the shining light. Her hair fell across her neck and down to the tops of her breasts. What color did she call it? Chestnut? Auburn? How could I let that moment go to waste?

I reached over and turned her face to mine. I kissed her. Her lips were stiff. She was still pretending to still be mad at me. Okay, I thought, I'll play this game. I'll jump through this hoop. I kissed her again, soft, and sat back in my seat. She sat up and turned to me.

Can you be a good boy?

Bring me your lips.

I mean it, you're not allowed to be mean to me.

I get it. Shut up and kiss me.

Her lips opened for my tongue and her hand reached down in my jeans. She started to move her hand. I drew a deep breath and held it. Laura put her hand over my mouth and looked at me.

We have to be quiet.

I slid my hand under her jacket and found her breast. Her nipple rose under my palm. I unhooked her bra and pulled her jacket over my head. She is warm in my mouth. I circled her nipple with my tongue. She pulled my head from her breast. She buried her mouth into mine.

One of my hands was in her hair. The fingers of my other hand traced up her thigh.

You trust me?

She nodded her head.

I inched higher.

Still trust me?

Yes.

My fingers slid past the hem of her shorts and reached the wetness between her legs. She moaned into my ear.

I knew I couldn't trust you.

I reached into her panties and spread her open. She pushed her body against my hand. I nibbled on her shoulder. Hoping it would relax her, I wanted to make her come.

She pulled her hand from my pants and moved down low in her seat. Her hips were in motion with my hand. Each time I pushed my fingers inside her, her ass rose from the seat to push them in deeper. When I circled my thumb over her clit, a sound started in her throat.

I switched the rhythm of my hand, one moment soft, furious the next. She grabbed my hand and held it in place. Her body flinched and stiffened as she came. I kissed her just to muffle her moans.

She pulled my hand from between her thighs and brought my fingers to her lips. She tasted herself and then kissed me deep. She gave me a long, direct stare before she spoke to me.

Look, we can fuck, have fun, right, but that's all. I just lost my husband and I don't need to get tangled up with someone else. Get it?

It occurred to me that I might need this. A little playtime. Some chaos to break things up. It will keep Jackie off my mind. I kissed Laura's forehead.

No problem.

Good.

She pulled her jacket up to her nose and turned back to the window.

Horny and ready for release, I felt like I got the ass end of the deal. That was a problem.

Oscar rests his head on the foot of the bed, begging me to make it stop. Neither of us can sleep. I look over to the stack of tests on my desk. If I'm going to be up, maybe I should get some work done. No.

I tie the strings on my pajama bottoms and pull the comforter back. When I swing my feet to the floor, my toes reverberate with the sound from the apartment downstairs. The music is loud, and it sounds like a dirge pumped through a foghorn.

This kind of thing was eventual. I'm the only person over thirty in the whole building, and one of maybe five women. The rent is cheap and it's close to the school. That's what I told myself when I signed the lease. I don't remember partying like these kids when I was in my twenties. I guess debauchery can look like the best option when it seems like the world is blowing apart.

Other than that, I love the place. It was built just after the turn of the century, and it's got lots of wonderful little touches. When the weather is nice, I can sleep in and ride my bicycle to work. On most days I walk.

But lately, I haven't been sleeping well. Between my neighbors and my restlessness, it's been two weeks since I had a solid night of rest. I can only manage an hour or two a night and I have to masturbate just to get to the point where I can close my eyes. I'm like an alley cat in heat. On top of that, my skin's breaking out like a teenager. I don't know what's going on.

Poor Oscar. I'm sure the dog just wants peace and quiet. I reach over to the night table and pick up my glasses. I have to do something about this. I put my robe on, grab my keys, and pull my hair back out of my face. The mirror by the door reflects a woman I don't recognize. How did I get this old?

I don't realize I'm barefoot until my apartment door shuts behind me. I look at the hallway carpet and make believe it's clean. It's just a few steps to the stairway, and my neighbor's apartment is at the bottom step.

As I get closer, I can identify the music. It's some kind of goth metal. I stop in the middle of the stairs. What am I doing? Is this smart? Is this safe? When did I become so afraid?

I can't allow other people to disrupt my life. I take a breath, walk the last few steps, and knock on the door. Nothing. I bang my open palm against the solid wood.

The door swings open and there is a naked woman standing in front of me. No, not standing, she's holding herself up against the wall. She's at her door, cockeyed drunk and naked.

Yeah?

I'm frozen, struck still by my amazement. She's pretty. She's tall and lean and I can't avoid noticing she's waxed recently. Blood quickly fills my face and pounds in my ears. I can't turn away. Thank God she can't see that I'm blushing.

Could you turn it down?

Sure.

I open my mouth, for what, to say thank you, to flirt, to lecture? I don't know, because just as quick as she appeared, she disappears and the door clicks shut.

My bare feet are cold on the worn carpet, and now I'm sure I won't be getting any sleep tonight.

Stretched out on my bed eating a rotisserie chicken and watching the Simpsons, I realized that since I visited Emily I have made a seamless transition back to bachelorhood.

We had a good week together. We talked about things before I left. We agreed the distance was a problem, but it was worthwhile to see if we could turn this into a real relationship. Over the weeks the phone calls became less frequent. Those were replaced by emails. They haven't become texts yet. That's next.

And my writing? It's going well. I just don't know where my life is going. It's time for some serious reflection. I'm 30 years old. I'm semi-employable. I have boozed my way through my early adult years. My nearest goal is striping the meat off this bird. My furthest horizon is my next piece of pussy.

My father told me I was headed for this. If he were still alive, I'd tell him it's not a bad life. He would say I'm just lazy. He might not go as far as shiftless. I don't think he would see the irony of using a loaded word like lazy. My father was an old school civil rights "colored" man. He fought a culture of racism by becoming the anti-nigger. Bill Cosby with a briefcase.

I get out of bed. I walk over to the desk and turn on my laptop. I wipe my hands on my sweatshirt and start typing. This is what comes out:

There's a gun in the closet. Two actually, a .45 and a 9mm. They're loaded. If only I had the courage to use one of them. I would save everyone a lot of trouble. The rounds are hollow points, or spreaders. I'm not sure. I know they'll rip a gaping hole through the back of my head. The bullet will hit the roof of my mouth and the tip will blossom like a mushroom. The force of the blast will expand to about the size of a large grapefruit. That's only if I use the 9mm. If I use the .45, they'll be lucky if my face is salvageable. My eyes will burst. My jaw will unhinge. My sinuses will explode through the hole where my nose used to be.

I can see and feel this experience clearly in my mind, without horror or fear. The courage, no, the commitment, required for the act just isn't there. Besides, suicide is such stupid, selfish, and boring. But the commitment, that's admirable.

A few years ago one of those stalker ex-husband types walked into a supermarket armed to the teeth. He killed his ex-wife and a state trooper. He was tried and convicted. This kind of story is in the news at least once a month somewhere in this country. Nothing about it is especially exceptional. Except for what happened next.

The guy didn't get a death sentence. While waiting to be sent to the state penitentiary, he killed himself. When they found him dangling by his neck, his arms were slit from wrists to elbows.

How many people do you know believe in something so thoroughly? Imagine pushing your head through the small bed sheet noose hanging against the cell door, splitting your forearms open with a dull, crudely fashioned knife, and then letting your body go limp. That's commitment. One man had a commitment to justice that twelve reasonable citizens couldn't muster.

That's my problem, a lack of commitment.

I've gotten off to some fine starts, only to neglect things and let them wither. Quitting would be an improvement. At least I would be committing to being a loser. Maybe if I dedicate myself to being a drunk. That would be a hell of a lot more palatable than this inertia. It's soul entropy.

I certainly can't commit to killing myself. So, what's ahead? Years of regret, bitterness, and isolation? What a fucking nightmare.

Soul entropy. Everything has its own energy and momentum. What happens when a soul nears the end of it's original impetus? When life is used up. If things continue as they are, I don't see any reason to continue.

I push my chair back from my desk. I read it. I need to pick up the phone and call someone. Stevie, Emily, anybody. Maybe go to a movie. A drink wouldn't hurt either. First, I need to finish that chicken.

This headache has been hammering me for five days now. I'm living on a cocktail of Tylenol, aspirin, and caffeine. I don't have health insurance, so a doctor is not in my future. The phone rings. I thought I unplugged that thing.

Yeah?

What ya doing hot stuff?

I feel like shit Laura.

Let me come over. I'll take care of you.

I won't be good company. I'm sure I'll end up saying something to piss you off.

C'mon, a little soup, maybe a snuggle?

Really, I don't think it's a good idea.

What's wrong?

Fuckin' headache. I can hardly see.

You need to lay down, rest.

That's what I was trying to do.

Okay grumpy, call if you need anything.

I swear, I never know what to expect with this woman. She can swing from sweetheart to bitch in record time. Except, of course, when she gets what she wants. I pull the line out of the phone and fall back into the sheets.

Someone's knocking on the door, and I curse to myself.

I can't catch a fuckin' break today.

Laura is standing there with grocery bags in her hands. Goddamn it.

Ta da!

I told you I was trying to sleep.

That was four hours ago. Boy, you really are sick.

I just want to be left alone.

Don't be silly. I went out and bought you all this good stuff. You could let me in.

She pushes her way past me.

Do what you want, I'm going back to bed.

I got just the thing for you.

I lay back down and Laura starts fiddling around in the kitchen. A couple minutes later, she comes in the bedroom balancing a bowl in her hands.

You need some food. Do you like tomato soup?

I can't remember the last time I ate, or what it was.

Hmmm, this is good.

Thank you. Here, take these too...

What is it?

It's some painkiller I had left over.

What is it?

Codeine, Percocet, I'm not sure.

She drops three pills in my hand. How old is this shit? One should do the job without doing too much damage. I throw it in the back of my mouth, and hand her back the others.

That's it?

If I need more than that, take me to the hospital.

Finish your soup and get some sleep. I'm going to clean up. Is it okay if I stick around?

I don't answer her. I just lay down and pull the sheet over my head. My head is bothering me too much to really think about anything.

I wake up, the sheets are soaking wet and the place is dark. There is light coming from under the bathroom door. I swing my feet off the bed and listen to her chopping and snorting lines.

Laura?

She pops out of the bathroom, stark naked.

You're up!

Yeah, um, what's the deal?

You feel better? Wanna play?

I do feel rested, and the headache is gone, but my brain feels fuzzy. My mouth is dry and my tongue feels stuck to the roof of my mouth. I look at her body. What was I trying to say?

What were you doing?

Come on, it's just a little blow. Don't get all Republican on me.

You can do what you want, it's your body, but I don't want that shit in my home. How many times do I have to ask you to respect my space?

You know what Steve, fuck you. I came over here and took care of your ass. The least you can do is thank me.

She's up in my face and the scent of her skin comes over me like a wave. I start to getting hard.

You're such a motherfucker, you know that. So what, I do a couple bumps in your bathroom. Fucking grow up!

You need to calm the fuck down.

She shoves me.

What are you going to do about it? Huh?

She pushes me again. I jump out of the bed, grab her arms, and pin her against the wall. The back of my thumbs sink into the soft flesh of her tits. I look into her wild eyes.

Chill. Just fucking calm down. Okay?

Fuck you.

Okay, you need to leave.

I let go of her and turn back to the bed.

Fuck off!

Her fingernails rip across my back.

Fucking bitch!

I turn around and raise my hand just above my shoulder. I freeze. I see myself standing in front of this nude woman. I'm shocked at the cliché of the whole thing. Her eyes are locked on my hand. They shift to my face.

Go ahead. Do it.

What? Did she actually just say that? What is happening?

What, you need my permission? Hit me. You know you want to.

This is insane.

Little punk bitch.

I slap her. The pop of our skin, my open hand against her cheek, snaps in the air between us.

Laura runs at me, fingers aimed for my face. I try to side step her, but her momentum knocks both of us to the floor. I wrap her up in my arms and squeeze her against me to keep her from scratching the hell out of me. We make low grunting sounds as we struggle. She's on top of me and I've got my legs scissored together to keep her from trying to knee me in the nuts. I roll us over and get her under control.

Stop! Fucking stop!

She keeps squirming and gets an arm free. She grabs the back of my head and pulls my face down to hers.

Fight me or fuck me, or let me go.

Laura's teeth flash at me just before she swings. She connects under my chin and the dark room flashes bright white for a second. It feels like a police siren ripping through my skull. This boiling thing erupts, and I swing back. My fist makes a connection that turns her head. She pushes air in and out between her teeth. She growls at me and tears off my boxers.

Let's go, c'mon.

I'm inside her. She's swinging both hands at me and I'm fighting to hold her down. She clubs me in the ear and I tumble off her. She pushes me down and mounts me. I cover my head as she keeps flailing at me. I open my eyes and see her bouncing on top of me. The only thing left to do is lay down and take it.

Fuckyoufuckyou...fuhfuhfuck...fuck...fuck...

I don't know if she comes or just wears herself out. She falls off me and props herself against the wall.

There is nothing I can say. This is a brand new world. I lay on the floor and listen to our breathing.

I finally met the piece of work that twisted up Stevie in Vegas. I had her pegged the second she walked into the bar. You couldn't miss her. She's a cut above the regular velveteen booze bags in this place. You see women just like her. God help you if you know one.

She's the one with the strong neck and cheek bones. A perfect ass. The one with the tiny hole in her eyebrow where there used to be surgical steel. She's well scrubbed and fashionably shabby. She knows life is her playground. She smells like reality, but will never stink of it. Her. Yeah, her. She was the only grown woman in a bar full of children.

There's something about strong women. They're irresistible up until the point they flake out. Or push you too far. Stevie didn't have a fucking chance. I wanted to have his revenge for him. I wanted to have her. I wanted to fuck her just for the story. I did end up with a story, but it didn't turn out how I thought.

Laura says she didn't know who I was when she perched herself on the barstool next to me. I don't buy it. Stevie must've told her about this place. I decided to act dumb and let her make her play.

She ordered a vodka, neat. She raised the glass to her lips and sipped. She lowered it and turned her entire body towards me. I could feel her gaze drilling through me. This was not going to be some flirtatious little chat.

I've known a dozen men like you.

I looked over at her. She had her glass back to her mouth. She lowered it and spoke again. This time she was looking at my reflection in the mirror behind the bar.

You think you're something special. You're not. You're a borderline alcoholic with some kind of Bukowski delusion. You make these little girls believe you hate women and you call it seduction. Really, you're desperate for someone to take you in her arms and tell you that you're a good man, that the world would be a better place if it just loved you like she does.

She was calm when she said all this. Her tone reminded me of a bored professor or a civil servant on a Friday afternoon. She took another sip and continued.

The truth is, you're clueless. Fumbling through your expensive education and a handful of genuine experiences, trying to find some kind of meaning. You're just another lost fool.

There it was. She laid it all out. Our surroundings only served to support her. The smoke soaked wood, the beer stained tile, the worn pint glasses, all gave witness. Somehow, she knew the truth of me. There was only one thing I could think to say.

Wanna wrestle?

She smiled. Half an hour later we were twisted up on my living room rug. She ended up on top of me, holding me down while I was inside her. There was no kissing. There was no gentle warm up. I've had angry fucks before. This time I was on the receiving end. Laura burrowed right through my mental and physical core. All I could do was hang on for the ride. I would worry about my emotions later.

Do you believe in good and evil?

What?

You know, good and evil. The idea that there are two forces are at work in the world, in constant conflict with each other. Good and evil. Do you believe in it?

Yes.

Tell me why?

Well, in the face of all the horror in the world, you have to believe there's something that stands against it. Yeah.

So it's more of a hope than an actual belief?

Sure, I guess. And you?

There is only human behavior and its consequences.

What about Morality??

My morality is based in self interest. I try not to do anything that I wouldn't want done to me.

What about that farm girl, Cassie?

That was completely her choice.

It suited your needs.

It was the best thing for everyone. You know, Cassie never bothered to ask me. I didn't know about it until after the fact.

And what measure of responsibility belongs to you?

My primary responsibility is to me. Thankfully, she feels the same way.

Really?

You trying to say something Stevie?

Nothing, forget it.

Don't preach to me. What about you and Ms. Las Vegas?

That's consensual.

Just because she likes getting slapped around doesn't make it right.

So you do believe in right and wrong...

Like I said, I wouldn't do anything that I wouldn't want done to me. Besides, right and wrong are not the same as good and evil. For example, it's only right that you buy the next round. It would be wrong if I had to ask you.

It looks like a quiet night until the estrogen patrol walks in. Gina, Mandy, and Cassie are suited up for manhunting. Decked out in tank tops, tight jeans, mini skirts, and baby doll t-shirts, they look more like trophies than hunters. They must be simultaneously dropping eggs. It never ceases to amuse me how shackled we are to our basic animal drives.

I've been bar tending for about five years. I've spent the last year here at the Thin Man. We get a good mix of people here. There are no televisions and no bottled beer. We pour draft beer, mixed drinks, and wine. There's cheap PBR for the hipsters. Our regular customers have jobs, and the liqourati keep coming back because we pour em straight up and play good music.

I serve the ladies their Cosmopolitans and then find something to occupy myself with at the other end of the bar. It's better to just stay out of the way when those three are together. Paint it up however we like, we're still just furless beasts. Some more than others.

It takes me a few seconds to place her, but one of Joe's lady friends walks in. She pulls back a stool and sits. She takes off her coat and knots her hair into a ponytail. Then I remember her. Laura, vodka neat.

I pour her drink and ask how she is. She swallows it back and looks at the bottle in my hand. I pour her another. She stares silently at one of the many Virgin Mary's behind the bar. Clearly, she wants to be left alone, preferably, with the vodka bottle. I go back to the end of the bar. I take the bottle with me. She knocks the bottom of her empty glass on the bar to call me over to pour her another. I think I might have to cut her off. Before I lift the bottle, she asks me a question.

Tony, are you married?

Nah.

Don't ever do it Tony.

How long you been married?

Too long.

You're a beautiful woman, I hope you didn't settle for less than you deserve.

She raises her glass, waiting for me to pour.

That's the kind of thinking that keeps getting me into trouble.

This last one's on me. Want some advice?

Is that gonna be free too?

I take the glass from her hand and set it back on the bar. I pour her shot and put the bottle back in the rack.

Some people aren't worth the trouble. You might be better off alone. At least for a little while.

It's not always easy. Sometimes life gets in the way.

She's right. Besides, it doesn't pay to argue with a drunk and miserable woman. You can keep that kind of trouble. I light her cigarette and bring her a clean ashtray. The three girls settle their tab and go off somewhere else. Laura sits alone staring at her drink and now I can have a smoke of my own.

My bohemian barroom days were coming to an end. It was time for me to find a job. Defeat, defeat, defeat. In a world of counterfeit and fractional men, defeat is the only cure. How a man responds to defeat is his measure. Take away whatever fuels him, and watch him respond.

The idle playboy days are over too. Emily reminded me last night that there's no such thing as a broke boyfriend. Not in her world. Thing's were fine when all I wanted was a good drunk. The drunken monk routine gets dull after a while. Human social interaction is moving up my list of needs. A social life requires money. Anyone who tells you different is a lying ignoramus.

The retirement fund/unemployment well has run dry. It's time to either work day labor or go back to customer service. It's death on either side. The only real choice is quick or slow.

This is how I found myself sitting in the day labor office, wondering how broke I want to be. I once knew a woman who lived in fear of poverty. She didn't understand the difference between being broke and being poor. Broke is temporary. There's always money to be made. It's just a matter of what you're willing to do for it.

This is the lie I tell myself as I sit surrounded by the fumes of cigarette smoke, stale sweat and used wine. The men around me look broken and spent. I tell myself I'm no different.

There's more to it of course. I'm here because I need a test. I suspect the fat internet years may have turned me into one of the soft fractional men that dominate our times. Men without guts, men of leisure and privilege. This is not a club I'm eager to join. My instincts have dulled. The street has new lessons to teach.

So I fill out all the government forms and legal waivers. Two hours later I'm waiting to be sent to a construction site. Some guy on the back bench has passed out. He smells like yesterday's malt liquor. The man sitting next to him keeps yammering away. He's having a conversation with nobody. A third man keeps to himself. He doesn't need to say much about himself. His life is right there for anyone who knows how to read a man. He hasn't been sober long. The train wreck of his life is at the bottom of his next bottle. It's the monkey's dilemma; surrender to base human needs or struggle to rise above them. I like him right away.

Who the hell am I kidding? Twenty years ago, yeah, I would have jumped right in and picked up a shovel, hammer, whatever. I've seen my hard time and I've busted my ass to not have to live like that again.

I get up and go home. Time to sharpen my resume and bust out my khaki's and button down shirts. Time to call the temp agency.

I still don't know if I passed or failed that one.

There is blood in my mouth.

This woman I just met is sitting next to me at the bar. She's saying something, what, I have no idea. Her lips, nothing like Laura's lips, are moving without sound.

Laura and I started this morning in each other's mouth. It's a good way to start the day. She has taught me a few tricks. When we finished I suggested we walk down the street for some drinks.

So we dress. No shorts and flip flops like the rest of the bums in this town. She wore this some kind of wrap dress thing that makes me just want to bend her over. I couldn't keep my eyes off her. Before we left, she pulled a vodka bottle and two shot glasses from the cabinet and sat down at the kitchen table. I am a lucky man.

Let's do battle with the Russians.

She pours each glass to the lip. I sit down like a good dog and I drink my shot. She drinks hers, and pours us each another.

Stevie, you're a lot of fun.

Thanks.

I am staring at her tits because she's not wearing a bra. She raises her glass and waits for me. We put that one down and her tongue chases the little bit at the corner of her mouth.

My husband is not dead.

She holds a steady gaze on me and pours two more shots.

I think it's important you know the truth, you know, before things get complicated. There was some ugliness the last time he caught me cheating. I had to make some promises to get him to take me back, and I don't think he'll let me get away with it a second time.

Does he know?

No, he travels. A lot. I keep the house, spend his money, and hang out with you. I'm sorry I lied to you.

Her hair is knotted behind her head. Her neck sweeps down to her shoulders in a strong, graceful line. She puts a cigarette in her mouth and lights it. How could a woman so beautiful be so poisonous? She exhales and looks at me through the smoke.

I lift my glass and pour it into my mouth. I let it sit there until it burns then I swallow.

The point is hon, I'm not going to leave him, but I want us to still see each other. If you can forgive me, that is.

She leaves it at that. Silence is definitely her best weapon. Like an expert salesman, she drops her offer and leaves it to me to pick it up. So, I'm supposed to be the other man. She's right, this isn't about infidelity. It's the lie between us that can fuck things up. We've been doing this dance for most of the summer. We can't go backwards and erase it all. I don't think it would've changed anything if I knew the truth from the beginning. Her lying to her husband, I don't care too much about that. Apparently, neither does she.

I can't be that guy Laura.

She reaches over and drinks her shot.

I appreciate you admitting the truth now, but I can't do it.

She picks up her stuff, and goes to the door.

That's it then. I won't be coming back.

She stands there. I'm waiting for her to go, but I guess she needs the goodbye to be complete. I walk over to her and take her face in my hands. We kiss goodbye. It's soft and it's short.

Sweet Stevie.

She looks at me. I know better, but I think she looks a little sad. This is her last ploy. She conjuring the illusion that I'm breaking her heart. The truth is, this was never about love. This was nothing more than the old-fashioned slap and tickle.

When she closes the door behind her, I want to run down to the bar. I need to be obliterated and I don't want to be alone.

I shower, shave, and do my best to make my misery look like detached cool.

A block from the bar, a woman gets out of her car and we make eye contact. She's pretty. I give her a smile and she smiles back. She heads down the sidewalk in front towards me and the bar. Before she turns in, some goon walking the other way makes a comment to her. She looks back at him. Her expression is a mixture of anger, fear, and surprise. She hesitates before she walking into the bar, perhaps to tell him to go to hell, but she goes in without saying anything.

Next thing I know, this mullethead walks right into me. We exchange words, nothing more than testosterone bullshit. He punches me in the face; I slug him in the gut. One, two, just like that. He's on his knees trying to breathe and I'm checking my nose for blood.

I leave him there and walk into the bar where Tony already has a whiskey waiting for me.

It's from the lady.

I raise the glass in her direction and swallow it back in two great gulps. I feel better immediately. The afternoon progresses and I make my way down to her end of the bar. What does Joe say? The best cure for bad pussy is new pussy? This one is named Donna. By the time the bar begins to fill with the after work crowd, we are real cozy. When we start making out, Tony gives us the fish eye because we're scaring the respectable clientele. We take a break and order another round.

I think about how drunk I am and my mouth feels like it's filling with warm wetness. Am I drooling? She points at me. I touch my lips with my fingertips. They're dark red. I move to stand up and everything goes gray.

Excuse...

An explosion blows through my skull and I feel like I'm falling. I get no sense that I'm ever going to hit the floor. Then, there's nothing.

Stevie, I know you've heard this a thousand times...

What?

Sexual success with women...

Depends on one thing: not fucking it up. I know.

Do you? All these guys in here think they have a chance with some of the women in here because the believe they understand that basic principle. Look around you, how do they seem to be expressing it?

Why don't you tell me?

I see a bunch of men standing in front of women, silently nodding their heads and smiling. It's a bar full of bobbleheads.

Some of them are going for humor as well.

Nothing but empty noise. It's better to sit in a block of uninterrupted quiet. It exerts a little pressure.

So, what's it mean to not fuck it up?

Not fucking it up is about asking questions, paying attention, and having a relevant thought or experience to what she says.

I'll get the next round, what are you drinking?

More of the same.

Sounds reasonable, but there are problems with that idea. First, it's a short term strategy. Second, it implies that women have a low level of expectation. As if they only want us around to make them feel good about themselves. We need to be able to bring more to the table.

Are you sitting at this bar because you've got the next 20 years of your life mapped out?

No.

You'd be a fool if you were. We're all in here to satisfy short-term needs. The point is, your priorities shape your approach.

What about my second point?

Well, that's the great thing about human social interaction.

What?

Self-involvement.

His stare was fixed on his coffee cup. His eyes, shaded by the brim of his baseball cap, were hollow. No emotion or thought seemed to light them. I could not take my eyes off him.

I was a wreck. My guts felt blown out. If I had been paying attention instead of obsessing over my loneliness, I would have seen her looking at me for the first time.

I was at home grading papers and my dog Oscar would not leave me alone until I took him for a walk. It was a good day to get out. The late fall afternoon was warm, and I was tempted to sit outside of my favorite bar and sip a Manhattan or two. When I turned into the coffee shop instead, I found myself staring at this man. For two weeks, whenever I went in there, he would be alone at that same table. Then, out of the blue, he asked to sit with me.

By the time I decided to speak to her, I had noticed a couple of things about her. The piles of papers she occasionally brought with her told me she was a teacher. Her dog was a big goofy looking retriever. It was crazy about her. She took good care of herself. Three days a week I'd see her run past the coffeehouse. Her long dreadlocks were always pulled back and draped over her shoulders, never covering her face. Her cocoa colored skin was clear. Her eyes were direct. I was driving a regular shift and had a few dollars in my pocket. I was feeling good. We had a good conversation.

he first conversation was typical. We talked about work, family, growing up, the basics. I looked at his pale, shaved, head and listened to him tell his tale. I was watching myself as well, waiting for warning signs. There was something different about him, as if a light had been turned on inside him and it's beam focused on me though his grey/green eyes.

She gave me her phone number and we talked about meeting again.

I gave him my number and waited for him to flake out.

I called her that weekend. We met for early drinks at her favorite bar. It turned out we knew some of the same people. I knew her ex-husband. I told her I knew him from around campus. The truth was he dated one of my ex-girlfriends. Sometimes this town is much smaller than it should be. She was cool about it. We drank a toast to the our incestuous little circle. Then, the night just got weirder.

When I found out that he knew my ex-husband, I didn't run screaming into the night. His eyes were soft and curious and they never left my face. We were talking about art. As I was explaining why I think still life paintings generally are crap, this drunk older woman walked up behind him and gave him a hug. I couldn't help but laugh at his look of surprise and the big lipstick kiss she left on his cheek. He managed to pull away and politely ask her to go away, but she wasn't taking no for an answer. He offered to buy her a drink and we escaped.

I was lightheaded when we got outside. Snow was just starting to hit the sidewalk. She reached up and wiped lipstick off my cheek. Her face looked like it was glowing, but she looked a little sad. I had to kiss her. Her lips were soft. I melted in them.

When he reached out and kissed me, I didn't hesitate. It felt right. It felt good. I could feel him breathe me in. He held my face gently, and his tongue traced inside my lips. I stopped to look at him and his eyes were still closed. A snowflake was on one of his eyelashes. He told me he wanted to take me back to his apartment and make out like teenagers. It was an obvious line, but I was ready to go home with him. Instead, I told him I couldn't. I had to go home and take care of Oscar.

I walked her to her car and went home with her scent on my hands and in my nose. I knew I was in trouble.

When he called me the next day, my first instinct was to screen him and play phone tag. I took the call.

We talked for over an hour. She enjoyed reading. She really loved teaching. She talked about her experiences overseas. Traveling seemed to be her way of discovering and pushing beyond her limitations. Life seemed to have left her slightly damaged, but wiser because of it.

I cannot tell you how wonderful it was to talk to a man who cares more about art than the sports pages. This town is loaded with so many pre literate metrosexual neanderthals. I had given up on meeting someone who's soul hasn't been eaten by men's magazines. He wasn't one of those effete hipsters either. He works hard, supports himself while going to school, and knows the difference between Manet, and Mamet. I listened and kept thinking about his lips. I knew the next time I saw him I'd have to get him naked.

I was relaxing on the couch and she called me wanting to go out. It sounded like a good idea. I got to her house and she was still getting ready. She came out wearing a short skirt and a some kind of hoodie sweater that was open down to her cleavage. She was ready to play. I started to stand up and she pushed me back down in the chair. She was straddling my lap before I could speak. She told me she had something to give me. I could feel the heat from between her legs. I reached around her skirt and felt her ass. Not yet, she said as she pulled my hand away.. She stood up and knelt between my legs. She looked into my eyes and opened my jeans. She wrapped her lips around me, and her mouth was the definition of warm and wet. She stopped to pull her dreds out of her face and did this thing where she tied them behind her head. She knew what she was doing and she took her time doing it. I covered my mouth to hold in a moan, and her scent was on my fingers. I was ready to bend her over and take her right there. And then she stopped.

I told him that was just the beginning of a long night, and if he could hang, he would never forget it. I wanted to see if he was man enough to wait. He just laughed kinda low, and told me not to let my mouth write a check that my ass couldn't cash. We got ourselves together and left for the bar. When we sat down, I was impressed that he pulled out the chair for me. Some people at the end of the bar raised their glasses at him and his little blond came bouncing over and kissed his cheek, but I didn't pay it any mind. I just knew that after getting some of my sweetness, he was going to be mine. We sat and flirted with each other over a couple of drinks, and I didn't give it another thought. I should've paid more attention. I got up to go pee and leaned over the table to kiss his ear, giving him a clear view down my shirt. I looked back over my shoulder on my way to the bathroom, and he was watching me walk away. When I was done, I was surprised to see him waiting for me outside the bathroom. Caught up in the charge of the night, I invited him in. He locked the door behind him and took me up in his arms. We kissed deep. He was sweet and gentle. I pushed him against the counter and turned my back to him. I pulled up my skirt and bent over. He crouched down, grabbed my hips, and put his mouth on me. He didn't hesitate. I think he was trying to tease me. It just made me hotter. My knees buckled, and I started to feel a rush of orgasms build inside me. I wanted to explode.

We paid our tab and ran back to her place. I didn't know sex could be that intense. We fucked for thirty straight days.

Most men can't keep up with me sexually. I usually end up feeling ashamed and slutty because of it. This man had stamina, and sex with him felt good like it's supposed to. It was like that for about a month then things started to change.

I felt like a crushed out 8th grader. Once, standing in line at the movies, I caught myself staring at the back of her head. The strands of her black and gray dreads spun as she turned to look at me. She had a wild, shining, look in her eyes and she smiled at me. At that moment, everything felt possible. I had fallen in love with her. I'm not talking about marriage, mortgage, kids, and the depressing ever after. Those are small dreams. I'm talking about everything. Everything felt possible

One night we were driving, taking in the sights of Colfax, and, for no other reason than the thought of his hands on my body, I was wet. I wanted him to touch me. I wanted his fingers on me, inside me, caressing me. I unbuckled my seat belt, turned towards him in the front seat of his cab, and opened my legs. He opened his mouth, looked at my hands touching myself, and stopped the words on his tongue. I just grinned back at him.

I was comfortable. Now I know, too comfortable. Nothing this woman did made any of my alarms go off. She wasn't there with me though. She was still in playtime mode. I was okay with that. I'm not looking for a wife. Besides, if she can't recognize what's standing right in front of her, what would I really be losing? We were either going to reach that next level of comfort or a place that felt like a wall. I waited and watched.

One night I had woken up from a strange nightmare. Oscar was falling apart in my arms, his tail, his legs, his snout were sliding off him. I had him bundled up in a sheet, and he was still alive. He was still alive, and there was no blood, he was just a pile of dog parts in my arms. I walked down the street sobbing for help. He pulled up in his cab and took the dog from me. We got in the cab and he told me we were going to a party. Everyone was dressed formally, and I was just in a slip. He took me over to the couch and a man was stretched out naked on it. He told me the party was for his friend, and that he was in a coma. Everyone circled around us and he told me that the only way this guy could wake up was if I had sex with him. I looked at all the people in their tuxedoes and cocktail dresses, and I straddled myself over this cold body on the couch. He was erect and inside me, and I could feel a chill spreading through my body. I moved up and down and everyone watched, waiting for me to come and bring him back to life. His eyes started to flutter, and the crowd started to cheer. I felt like I couldn't breathe, like my heart was going to stop, and I woke up. My heart was thundering in my ears, and my face was wet from crying. He was not in my bed. All I wanted was to have his arms around me, to hear his breath in my ear, and he wasn't there.

One night we were sitting at a stop light in my cab when a woman stepped into the crosswalk. The woman was no more, no less, beautiful than any other woman you might see walking down the street. Yet she was exactly the kind of woman that made other women fidget with their clothes. That's exactly what was happening in the seat next to me. The woman turned and smiled at me. We sat there in my cab. I could feel our insecurities, hopes, passions, and regrets surrounding us. I just kept breathing. That woman was in our field of view less than ten seconds, and now I know that moment was the beginning of our end.

The New Year's party and his little blonde friend Katia is what finished things for me. The night started off bad when he showed up late and was really distant with me. He kept giving me monosyllabic answers, and wouldn't make eye contact. I knew something was on his mind, but he's so closed. I figured he would open his mouth when he was ready. Then we go to this party and this girl he goes to school with, Katia, is all up in his face being sweet to him. It was like I disappeared. When they finally acknowledged my presence, she was wiping her trampy lipstick off him. He was suddenly in a better mood.

All said and done, I think the whole thing fell apart for three reasons:

The woman in the crosswalk reflected a much larger tension between us; she was always in an emotional state of looking over her shoulder, waiting for me to leave her for someone else. She would never let go of the idea that there was someone else out there who was better for me. "A perfect match", to use her words. We were drinking one night and she finally admitted she was waiting for me to leave her for a white woman. That kind of thinking comes from a lack of faith. She didn't have any faith in me, us, or most important, herself. If you asked her, she'd probably say it was because of reason #2:

My past. I've had relationships with more than a handful of women. Okay, more than two handfuls. Fuck it, more than my fair share. Some of them are still my friends. Yes, I'm that guy. I like women. With few exceptions, I prefer their company to men. As long as she can accept me as I am, and not try to train me into some twisted version of her father/prince charming, I'm cool with a woman. She was never comfortable with that. I couldn't tell you why, she just didn't dig the fact I had women friends.

Mostly, I think it all came down to the fact that I'm not an easy guy to be in a relationship with. I won't accept responsibility for anyone else's happiness. I won't soften who or what I am just to be likable. I'm horrible at compromise. She's a grown woman, she figured most of this stuff out for herself. I guess she thought she was able to handle it. Turns out, she wasn't. Or maybe she just wasn't willing.

After New Year's it was only a matter of time before things came to a head. I can't hang around in a relationship waiting for it to fall apart, so I just moved on. Why waste time explaining myself? Besides, if it really mattered to him, he would have made an effort right? There was no phone call, no email, no text, nothing. The man's a player, and real players don't know how to retire. They just change the game. Instead of bouncing from bed to bed, he would end up keeping someone on the side and giving me something that only resembled love. He couldn't handle what I have to offer

Even if none of that was an issue, we just didn't belong together. I mean relationships are hard enough, why pile the complexities of race on top of it all. It's just too much work.

I gave her some time and space. I stayed away from the coffee shop and kept my own company at home. The weeks passed and I didn't hear from her. I waited until I couldn't remember why I was waiting. I never saw or heard from her again. I'm okay with not knowing why things happen. I figure I got more than I lost in the whole thing. Besides, I really like drinking coffee by myself, in my kitchen, surrounded by the morning light.

WHAT ARE YOU DOING WITH YOUR LIFE!

I wake up face down in my own vomit to the voice of the madman on the street. I'm not trying to be poetic, there really is some nut wandering the neighborhood screaming. He's a regular. He walks around strumming his guitar vacantly and screaming at the top of his lungs. Today he's yelling the things a disappointed parent would say to a teenager.

CUT YOUR HAIR!

I'm glad to be awake though. Hell, I'm happy to be breathing. The puke is still moist, but some of it is caked in the corners of my mouth. It looks like last night's dinner. Yep, snow peas, shredded cabbage, and baby corn. I haven't been this shitty since high school.

GET A JOB!

Last night I found out that Stevie died. I was supposed to go on a date with the school teacher. I went to the bar instead. I invited her to join me but she wanted no part of it.

WHY CAN'T YOU BE MORE LIKE YOUR BROTHER?

Stevie is dead. I was at the end of the bar throwing 'em down. Walleyed and bitter, I scanned the crowd. Everyone in the place just made me angry. None of these faux ironic pampered twits could equal Stevie. Another lost chunk of American manhood.

YOU'LL NEVER GET ANYWHERE WITH THAT ATTITUDE!

I met Stevie in college. I was wandering the campus with my camera and interviewing random people for some long forgotten project. This kid was sitting reading in the dorm lobby. I asked him if it was okay for me to videotape him and ask some questions. Before I could turn on the camera he launched into how he was born and raised Boston, grew up on the cape, and transferred to school in Denver after a few years in Georgia. He told me he liked to travel, play poker, and read old detective novels.

He reeled all this out to me, unprovoked, and with a lot more detail than I'm telling you right now. He was itching for human interaction. I just let the camera roll. His openness and enthusiasm was exceptional.

We spent the rest of that afternoon talking over beers.

ONE DAY, YOU'LL THANK ME FOR THIS!

I should call the cops on this asshole. What kind of American would I be then? Citizen stool pigeon. I need to get my ass in the shower and clear my head. Maybe then I'll be able to deal with the puddle of puke. Looking at it makes me want to get sick again.

This is what happens when I drink Irish whisky all night. I could have been fucking the blonde I met last night instead of sleeping in Chinese food.

IT HURTS TO SEE YOU DO THIS TO YOURSELF!

I watched the three girls as they walked in and giggled their way up to the bar. They were dressed like MTV hookers. Hormones and culture mixed up and served cold. They looked like my kind of poison.

I watched some Johnny Hipster make his way over to lay his little game down. He offered to buy their drinks and they demurred. Strike one on the pimp approach. Next, he asked them if they could give him some advice. He switched to sensitive guy. Strike two. I swear, last week he was using a Scottish accent. Last night he told these women a story about how he met a woman who coaxed him into the bathroom to make out. He was starting to lose them. I could tell because the blonde was no longer paying attention. She was smiling at me over her drink. The next thing out of his mouth either took huge balls, or minimal brain cells. I sipped my drink and smiled back at the blonde.

He told the girls that this woman wanted to fuck right then and there but he couldn't get it up. Wait, here comes the punch line. Apparently, this woman, who was so drunk she was ready to get it on in the shitter, told him where she was going to be later in the evening and offered to meet him there if he changed his mind. He asked the girls if they thought he should go. They looked back at him in silence. This new playboy pose failed him as well. strike three.

The girls said they had no idea what he should do.

Maybe you should get a guy's point of view.

The blonde pointed at me. I looked at him. He looked like a complete non-threat. He was cultivating some kind of yuppie boho vibe - employed but not greedy. I chuckled.

I can't believe you just told that story.

What do you mean?

Look, even if it's true, why would you tell three beautiful women a story about how you couldn't get a hard on?

He was horrified. I had cock blocked him and blown his cover in one shot. Admittedly, he had done all the work. He acted like he had no idea what I was talking about. He was soon off in the corner by himself again. I introduced myself to the ladies and ordered another round.

The blonde's name was Cassie.

WHY DO YOU HANG OUT WITH THESE PEOPLE?

Stevie is dead. Stevie was afternoons watching the pretty girls over a cup of coffee. Stevie was nights at the end of the bar, telling lies, and making each other laugh. Stevie was my friend. I wish we could've had more time. I'm glad for the little I got.

YOU WON'T MAKE THE TEAM IF YOU DON'T APPLY YOURSELF!

I really should have stopped myself last night. I could've kept my mouth shut and closed the deal. Cassie could see I was on my way to annihilation. She suggested we go somewhere else. I suggested we walk down the block and play pool.

I was beyond reach before my third glass of Guinness. I told her about Stevie. I think she gave me her number. Everything after that is a haze.

WHEN ARE YOU MOVING OUT?

The last time I saw Stevie we walked through the park one nigh after leaving the bar. The sky was clear. The stars seemed bright. It was so cold the trees creaked and popped under the weight of a fresh cover of snow. When we got to his block, I just gave him a nod. He just waved. That was almost a week ago.

IS THAT THE BEST YOU CAN DO?

I've managed to clear the chunks out of my nose and from behind my ear, but I still feel like dried dog shit. I need to go lay down.

I cant do this.

I'm standing outside on the balcony and the rain is softly plink plonking into my glass of vodka. I'm at Stevie's wake in someone's apartment on Capitol Hill. It's a refurbished turn of the century building. Apartment lofts. At least they're not being torn down.

Then don't.

A woman is standing behind me, out of the rain. She's a short brunette with matter of fact eyes. Wait, that's not clear. Hers are the kind of eyes you look into and see a complete lack of manufacture. She has honest eyes. She's holding a towel. I turn back towards the sky.

That's good advice.

You should get out of the rain.

I suck at listening to good advice.

Please make sure your glass doesn't fall.

She waited a few seconds before saying that. Her voice sounds wounded, but not angry. The screen door clicks shut. I'm alone again. Good. This is one of my best skills: sending people away.

Except for Stevie. He would not go away. No matter how much of an ass I was. No matter how arrogant, drunk, or bitter I got. He was there. He always had something to do. If it was fun or free, or both, Stevie knew about it and would drag me out of my hole to do it. Sometimes it was a two for one happy hour, other times it was music in the park. It was always a good time.

Fuck. I pick the glass off the balcony rail and take two deep gulps. Fuck, fuck, fuck. The people inside are standing around talking about him. As if the act of remembering will somehow make it less painful. So many people need others in order to feel alive.

I can't do it. I can't embrace strangers and softly wish them well. I can't talk about, "do you remember that one time..." When I cry, I want to be alone. I can only vent my anger by punching something or someone. I don't know how to make my mourning a public thing. She's right. If I cant do this, I shouldn't.

I should go home, sit down at my desk with a glass of ice and a bottle of Irish whiskey, and write until the pages are wet with my tears. I should run home in the rain until the anger burns out of me. I should run until there is no difference between sweat, rain, and my weeping. I should.

Yet here I am. All I can do is be me. I turn around and look through the glass doors. People are standing around, shoulders slumped, arms crossed, heads down, hands over their mouths. I don't even understand the body language of mourning. The woman left a towel draped on the arm of a plastic patio chair. I step under the cover of the balcony overhead and put my glass down. I dry my head and hands. I scan the room.

The room's layout is a combination living room and dinning room. It's the result of limited space, money, and imagination. The kitchen is separated from the rest of the space by a large counter that is standing in as a bar. This is where Stevie's bike messenger friends are congregating. They're drinking heavily and they're the liveliest human specimens in the room.

Hovering around the couch in the corner are the post-urban, pre-breeding, college friends that didn't speak to Stevie frequently. This is where most of the crying is happening. Stevie's musician hipster friends huddle near the entrance to the room. In the center of the room, right where she should be, Laura is holding court. The group is collectively nodding their heads in agreement to something. I walk over to Laura and the bunch circled around her. I completely disregard what they're talking about.

I fucked a crippled girl once.

Quiet nervous laughter is the only response.

Actually, she wasn't a cripple, she just had a touch of the palsy.

Okay Joe, you're cut off.

It wasn't all that bad, all she had was a limp.

C'mon, you should stop now.

She was a good fuck too.

Someone spit out a chuckle.

That's it, let's go.

Laura grabs my arm and hustles me to the door.

Stay here.

I tilt my glass up to my mouth, emptying it. Look through the bottom, I can see that anyone who isn't flapping their lips is slackjawed and staring at me. Good. Now they've got a target for their anger and frustration. Besides God, that is.

Laura comes back with our coats and pushes me out the door. When we get downstairs and out to the sidewalk the rain is turning to snow. I hand her my empty glass.

I'm going home.

She clasps my hand around the glass.

You going to be okay by yourself Joe?

Yeah.

I'll call you later, okay?

You do that.

Let me start off by saying there's no such thing as just putting it in for a couple of seconds. In all the history of sex there is no greater delusion.

There are no choices in here!

Cassie was rooting around in her nightstand. She was straddled over me. Her nipples brushed against my chest. I looked past them to my stomach. I was getting a little flabby. I hadn't seen the inside of a gym in a while. Something needs to be done about that. I looked over at the open drawer and saw she had pulled out a tube of lube and was pushing a dildo out of the way. She mumbled something.

What are you looking for?

We're out of condoms.

This was the culmination of a twenty dollar date. Yes, a twenty dollar date. Not a booty call, but not quite a hookup either. Put this one your time capsules folks. At the open of the 21st century it was still possible to have a date in America and not spend more than $20. You got a decent bottle of wine, cab fare, and a box of condoms. What are going to do? Expectations were low. Everyone left behind by the new economy was screwing, or, screwed. But not me. Not tonight. Apparently. I spent a little extra money on a good bottle of wine and assumed my modern, liberated, fuck buddy would have her own rubbers. What single American hetero woman between 28 and 48 doesn't?

What do you mean we're out of condoms?

Cassie shrugged.

No raincoats Joe.

She steadied her gaze and wrapped her fingers around my cock.

You know, I just finished my period.

This is how it begins. No impulse control, no planning ahead. Next thing you know, you're somebody's baby's daddy. Oh boy.

Just make sure you pull it out, k?

Her eyes locked on my mine. She was taking her measure of me.

Sure, just for a couple seconds.

And I was in. I can count the women I've been inside this way on half a hand. It's a good feeling, better than most women's' mouths. Her strokes on top of me got shallower until she was just grinding against me. I kept running 80's pop songs through my head to distract myself. She came quickly, humming soft coos against my neck.

When I pulled out, I saw that I had already started to come. Yeah, this woman was beginning to be bad news.

What do you believe in?

I could see Joe was ready to launch some clever witticism from his tongue. Instead he looked at me and sipped his beer. I could see he was giving the question real thought. More than five minutes passed before he opened his mouth.

First and foremost, I believe in me and my abilities.

I believe everything happens for a reason, especially when it comes to people. We're just not always ready, or able, to see why.

He put his bottle to his lips and took a pull. He looked down into the bottom of it and kept speaking.

I believe most people are just plain lazy. The path of least resistance is well worn.

Good and evil are oversimplifications. Humans are more complex than that.

I believe in paying attention, planning ahead, and persistence.

I believe talent is not enough. You have to do the work.

I believe it's important to make an ass of yourself every now and then, especially when it comes to love.

I believe in reckless ambition.

I believe oral sex is the most intimate physical act.

I believe sense of humor is overrated.

Joe tips his head back and empties the bottle.

I believe nothing heals a broken heart like more pussy and another drink.

And Stevie I believe you should know better than asking me a question like that after I've had too much to drink.

I woke up this morning with three women on my mind. I called each of them and told them I wanted to see them. The possibility I was committing self sabotage didn't occur to me at the time. I might not be as smart as I believe.

I am asleep in my chair on the porch later that afternoon. With the heat, a few beers, and the ball game on the radio, you could say I am passed out. Which is why someone is tugging on my toe.

Rise and shine Mr. Sandman.

It's Emily. She's standing on the other side of the porch railing, her overnight bag in one hand and my foot in the other. This is a happy surprise. I didn't figure on hearing from back from her for at least a week. Especially since Emily travels as part of her job. I just left a message with her to be thorough.

I listen to her tell me how she got my message, juggled her flight schedule, and arranged for an overnight layover so she could see me. All the while, my eyes follow the line of her body until they come to rest on her painted toes. No use letting a long-distance booty call go to waste.

Soon we're getting sweaty on the sheets. We take each other like it's the last sex we're ever going to have. Afterwards, I grab us beers from the fridge.

I'm sorry I couldn't be here for you when Stevie died.

I hand her a bottle.

Things were strange with us. Did we ever actually break up?

Emily yawns.

No, but that's something we need to talk about.

Agreed. For now, just relax. I'll pour you a bath.

She fades to sleep by the time I get the tub clean. The sound of the water filling the tub almost drowned out the knocking on the door. For a moment, I think about not answering it. I know the knocking will only get louder. That would be worse than the alternative. I open the door. It's Laura. I let her in. Before she finishes telling it, I can imagine the whole scenario:

She called to give me the I'D LOVE TO, BUT. Laura is the queen of the I'D LOVE TO, BUT. I'd love to have drinks, but I'm busy. Suck your cock, I'd love to, but you're too big. (I wonder how many chumps believed that one). I can't think of anything more exciting than wandering around all night to stare at art, but... You get the picture.

After an hour of not getting through, she flipped into mother hen mode and came over to make sure I was okay. My cell phone must be off. We've played this game before. We've been at it long enough that it's become part of the secret language that makes two people a couple. Not that either of us would admit to it.

As she tells her story, she's sits on the couch with her legs crossed. Her ankle moves in a smooth arc as she bounces her leg. The hem of her sundress creeps up with each swing. I just know that lightweight cotton is the only thing between me and her ass. She has the look of a woman who knows she can have a man turning flips for her. She'd like them right now, thank you very much.

I've got company.

Yes you do.

Besides you.

She pulls a pack of smokes from her purse and lights one up. She's settling in. She narrows her eyes at me and exhales. Her leg, and the dress, stop moving. It's enough to make a man want to cry.

I'll be back.

I go into the bedroom and the bed is empty.

In here.

Emily is in the tub reading and sipping her beer.

Are you going to join me?

A friend stopped by. Feel like entertaining?

You go right ahead, I'm going to soak awhile.

I feel like a scumbag. I bend down and kiss her forehead. Guilt is working its way inside me, and I haven't done anything. Yet.

Back in the living room, Laura has stubbed her cigarette out and I can see her wide nipples pushing against the fabric of her dress.

Truth or dare.

Here we go. The gave have begun. I'll play along.

Dare.

Eat me.

I'm on my knees, gripping her ass, my face between her thighs, her dress over my head, before you can say complication. I'm not thinking. I'm going where the day leads me. By the time I slip my fingers inside Laura, she's arching her back and biting her lip. Now she's as sweet as pie. I open a bottle of red and she changes the radio station. Emily emerges from the bedroom and is scrubbed fresh. I have to say, I'd marry that woman if she'd have me.

After introductions, the two of them share a joint and act like old buddies. I can't believe my luck. I start to relax a little. I may as well dive in and swim while I can. Because sure as shit, I'm gonna drown.

The three of us knock back the first bottle and Laura opens another while I shower. We play cards and listen to the radio. We wait until the last of the sun seeps out of the windows before turning on a light. Emily passes out on the couch as Ray Charles is on the radio telling us all about love, careless love. I rub Laura's feet and start nodding off.

I drag myself to bed. Stick a post in the side of the road for this day. The memory of it will keep me warm when I'm old and alone.

I wake up later and open my eyes to see Cassie hovering over me. She's drunk and pulling my shorts off. I'm lost for a couple of seconds, but by the time she's got me in her mouth, I realize what's going on. Giving her a key was a mistake. This is what happens when she gets drunk and lonely.

It doesn't take long for her to climb on me. I'm drained but I feel like steel inside her. This won't be quick. That seems to be working for her, because she's taking her time. I reach up to tangle my fingers in her hair. My palms brush across Cassie's wet cheeks. She shakes my hand from her her head. She braces her arms against my chest and grinds into the final wave of her orgasm.

It's easier to ask for forgiveness than it is to ask for permission.

Ever heard this bullshit before?

Assholes like to use it to justify the unconscionable. They think they can erase all responsibility with an apology.

Go ahead, fuck that donkey. The owner won't like it, but he'll get over it. That kind of crap.

It's easier to ask for forgiveness than it is to ask for permission.

This is exactly what I tell myself the next morning. Emily is standing above me. Cassie is passed out by my side. I have no idea where Laura is.

Emily puts her hand on her hip.

I've a plane to catch. It doesn't look like you'll be able to see me off.

Em, I can't even begin to explain.

But you will. You owe me that much.

Right now?

Her eyes jump to Cassie's blonde hair splayed out on the pillow and then focus back on me. She's pissed.

Yes.

Emily turns and leaves the room.

I check on Cassie. She's asleep and breathing deep. I need to remind her not to come over without calling.

I can hear the sound of wheels on wet pavement outside my window. It's still dark. Who's on the road this early in the morning? Eager beavers and overachievers. Suckers, all of them. I slip out of bed and look at Emily in the kitchen.

Do we have time for coffee?

My plane leaves at seven.

I look over at the clock. The faint glow reads four am.

I shuffle into the bathroom to release what seems like an endless stream of piss. I run my hands under some water and make it to the kitchen. It's a mess. I need to find a cup, rinse the pot, clean out the filter, scoop fresh grounds into it, pour water into the machine, and turn it on. Fuck it. That's more focus than I can manage. I stand over the sink and stare at the wine dried in the bottom of last night's glasses.

This is life. Life is work. Every single moment of pleasure is punctuated by, surrounded by, built up by, work. What's wrong with me? I'm capable of being a good worker bee. I'm no different than the guy who belts up his khakis and heads to his beige/grey cubicle everyday. Yet, the whole process drains me.

Sure, I drink a lot. Maybe too much. Yeah, fucking is the only thing outside of writing that I'm interested in. But these are common distractions. They don't seem to keep Bob Khaki from sitting in front a spreadsheet all day.

I grab the note pad on the fridge and write Cassie a note.

Call me tonight.
I go back in the bedroom and stick the note to her forehead. A few minutes later I'm dressed and we're on our way to the airport. I'm driving. Emily loses her patience after we hit the highway.

I can't keep waiting for you to figure out what you want.

This is not about what I want. If Emily wanted to get married, I would happily do it. Without hesitation. No matter how bad that idea is. This is about what I'm capable of. I could lie and blame it on the distance. If I'm honest, I know it's more than that. I don't know how to say any of this to Emily.

I know what I want.

Really? Why on earth would you do what you did? What were you thinking? Were you even thinking at all Joe?

This is why a stable adult relationship is equivalent to celebrity. It sounds interesting until I think about it. Instead, I watch women pass in and out of my life . I am a rest area. That's no kind of an explanation. It's useless to try explaining a man.

I don't know.

I deserve better than this.

She's right. The apology starts in my throat but can't leave my tongue.

I'm tired of being the woman a guy has to lose before he gets his shit together. I'm done.

Emily turns away from me. Her body is twisted towards the passenger door. We pull up to the car rental depot. I've driven Emily to silence. She takes her bag from me before we board the shuttle. I sit next to her.

Muted tears flow down her cheeks. The other passengers are quiet as we rattle along. They alternate between avoiding us and glancing over. I feel confused. I know she's just broken up with me. I don't know how to act like that absolves me from being a good host. I walk with her through the terminal as far as the bridge to Concourse A.

I watch her walk down the conveyer. This is not supposed to happen. Not to me. Joe the bohemian playboy, that's me. I should be picking up the scent again. Flush out the next bird and don't look back. Instead, I am melancholic and overwhelmed. Sucker punched. I feel like a lost little boy.

Defeat. In a world of counterfeit and fractional men I can't think of a better cure. This moment is my medicine. How a man responds to defeat is his measure.

I stand watching her hair bounce as she walks away. All I have left are words. That's poverty compared to the wealth of the experience.

It's easier to ask for forgiveness than it is to ask for permission. Right.

There is a box on my neighbor's porch. It sits next to a green folding chair. It's brown cardboard with the top flaps folded in. It's big enough to hold a case of beer cans and bottles. He likes to sit out on his porch and listen to baseball on his radio. Sometimes he reads, sometimes he drinks. Mostly, he just watches the traffic go by. We don't talk much, he says hello once in awhile, and sometimes I sit on my porch and listen to the game with him. One day, a pretty blonde came by and shouted his name.

What?

She asked him why he isn't answering his phone.

I'm busy.

Yeah? What's her name?

He sipped his bottle of beer.

No. Why don't you just come clean with me Joe?

He got out of his chair and leaned over the railing.

I've been nothing but honest with you.

There's something I need to tell you.

Didn't you walk out of here a month ago telling me never to call you?

We need to talk.

You made this choice Cassie.

Can I come inside?

No.

Joe, I was pregnant.

I went inside my apartment. I was embarrassed for him. I left the screen door open so I could hear more.

As in past tense?

Why? Would you have done anything besides act like a coward?

His chair scuffed as he sat back down.

I couldn't count on you. I think this is best for everyone.

You're unbelievable. It's not like you even gave me a chance. What did you hope to accomplish by coming here?

I just thought you should know.

Come inside, we'll talk about it.

What else is there to say?

He asked her to come in again, and she told him she couldn't. He dropped his empty bottle in the box beside him and watched her walk back to her car. I didn't go back outside until I heard him open another bottle of beer.